Bible Legends

B·I·B·L·E
LEGENDS

An Introduction to Midrash

VOLUME ONE : GENESIS

LILLIAN FREEHOF

With introductions and commentaries by
HOWARD SCHWARTZ

Illustrated by PHYLLIS TARLOW

UAHC Press ◆ New York, New York

Talmudic references throughout this book are from
the *Talmud Bavli,* the Babylonian Talmud.

Library of Congress Cataloging-in-Publication Data

Freehof, Lillian S. (Lillian Simon), 1906–
  Bible legends.

  Bibliography: v. 1, p.
  Contents: v. 1. Genesis.
  Summary: A collection of Jewish legends focusing on such primary
characters of the book of Genesis as Adam and Eve, Noah, Abraham and
Rebecca, Jacob, and Joseph.
  1. Legends, Jewish.   2. Bible stories, English—
O.T. Genesis.   2. Midrash—Juvenile literature.
[1. Folklore, Jewish.   2. Bible stories—O.T. Genesis.
3. Midrash]   I. Schwartz, Howard, 1945–
II. Tarlow, Phyllis, ill.   III. Title.

BM530.F73   1987   [398.2]   87–13799
ISBN 0–8074–0357–1 (v. 1)

Contents

Introduction   ix

1♦ THE MOANING OF THE WINDS   1

2♦ THE WICKED BROTHER   13

3♦ THE BLUE SAPPHIRE BOOK   24

4♦ THE RAINBOW   37

5♦ THE WONDERFUL CHILD   45

6♦ THE GARDEN IN THE FIRE   53

7♦ THE SHELTERING CLOUD   66

8♦ JACOB'S BLESSING   78

9♦ JACOB AND THE ANGEL   92

10♦ THE STONES THAT BOWED DOWN   104

11♦ FROM SLAVE TO PRINCE   114

12♦ BROTHERS AGAIN   126

Selected Bibliography   143

Bible Legends

Introduction

In the Bible we are told that God gave the Torah to Moses on Mount Sinai. Those Jews who regard the Torah as the literal word of God believe that all truth can be found within it, if only its teachings can be fully grasped. Therefore, the rabbis devoted themselves to understanding every single biblical reference, often composing a story—a midrash—to elaborate on the biblical narrative.

What, for example, was the significance of the silver cup that Joseph had hidden in his brother Benjamin's sack? When Joseph's steward stops the brothers, the steward, as Joseph has instructed, says: *"It is the very one [cup] from which my master drinks and which he uses for divination."* (Gen. 44:5) This is the first and only indication that Joseph practiced divination—the art of reading the future—suggesting that magic may have been the source of Joseph's mastery of dream interpretation. For the rabbis, this single reference became the source of a tradition that viewed Joseph as a diviner and his cup as a kind of crystal ball.

In one of the stories in this book, "Brothers Again," the silver cup plays a more important role than it does in the Torah. In this ancient midrash, retold by Lillian Freehof, Joseph looks into the cup and pretends to see the future so he can surprise his brothers with all he knows about them. Up to this point there is no indication that the cup is magical. Then Joseph asks

Benjamin to look into the cup. As soon as Benjamin peers into it, he discovers that the prince of Egypt is Joseph his brother. Here, the cup is shown to be truly magical, and its existence serves to explain Joseph's uncanny ability to interpret dreams.

Determining the origin of the cup was itself a mystery that the rabbis sought to solve. Their solution made use of a "chain midrash" which associated the cup of Joseph with Adam, Noah, Abraham, Isaac, and Jacob. How this technique works will become clear as we resolve two other biblical mysteries.

At the beginning of Genesis it is written: *"God said, 'Let there be light'; and there was light."* But Genesis 1:16 teaches: *"God made the two great lights, the greater light [the sun] to dominate the day and the lesser light [the moon] to dominate the night."* Which of these lights, then, was created on the first day?

The second mysterious passage concerns Noah's ark. In the Torah it is written that light entered the ark by means of a *tzohar*. But the rabbis did not know the meaning of *tzohar*. Was it a window? That is how light usually enters a room. Remember, however, it rained for forty days and nights, keeping the ark dark. The rabbis wondered how those aboard Noah's ark could see what they were doing. Their only clue was the passage about the *tzohar*. Some of the rabbis decided that the *tzohar* was not a window but a magical source of light. Thus originated the legend of the glowing jewel known as the *Tzohar*, a legend that will help us discover the origin of the magic of Joseph's divining cup.

According to this legend, Noah hung a glowing jewel on the deck of the ark, and it cast enough light to illuminate the entire vessel during the days of the Flood. This midrash solved two mysteries. It defined *tzohar*, and it explained how the ark was lit.

Jewish legends tend to focus on such primary figures of the Bible as Adam, Abraham, and Moses; on such a famous rabbi as Rabbi Akiba; or on such persons, places, or objects that require explanation as the *Tzohar*. Once a legend like that of the

Tzohar is created, it is recalled time after time, for it has become a part of Jewish tradition.

Sometimes later legends attempt to answer questions raised by earlier ones. For example, what makes the *Tzohar* glow? The rabbis answered that its light was created on the first day when God said: *"Let there be light."* The light of the first day, called the primordial light, made it possible to see from one end of the world to the other. Most of this light disappeared from the world at the time of the Fall—after Adam and Eve disobeyed God and ate the fruit of the Tree of Knowledge. God, however, preserved the light inside a glowing jewel—the *Tzohar*—to remind Adam and Eve of all they had lost.

This legend about the primordial light solves another problem in the biblical text; it explains the difference between the light created on the first day and that created on the fourth. (The text appears to describe two separate creations of light.) Note how these two legends, that of the glowing jewel and that of the primordial light, complement one another: some light is preserved in the jewel, explaining why the *Tzohar* glows. However, another question remains unanswered: How did Noah acquire the glowing jewel? The rabbis answered this as well and, in the process, created another kind of legend known as a "chain midrash." Accordingly, the *Tzohar* was first given by God to Adam, who gave it to his son Seth, and it was passed down from father to son until it reached Methuselah. Methuselah gave it to his son, Lamech, who gave it to his son, Noah.

Nor does the legend end there. The glowing stone was passed on in this manner until it was handed down to Abraham, who wore it on a chain around his neck. The Talmud relates that anyone who was sick could look into the stone and be cured. In this legend, then, the stone not only provides light but also has the power to heal. Abraham gave the jewel to Isaac, who gave it to Jacob, who, in turn, gave it to Joseph. When Joseph was cast into the dark pit, the jewel provided him with light. Joseph brought the jewel to Egypt and placed it inside the silver cup. That is how Joseph was able to divine when he looked into the cup.

Thus we come full circle, back to Joseph's cup, which is linked to all the key figures in biblical history. But the story did not stop there. Once a vivid tale came into being, it continued to appear in different guises. The *Tzohar,* for example, was found by Moses in the coffin of Joseph, which was summoned by Moses from its burial spot at the time of the Exodus from Egypt. Moses hung the glowing jewel in the Tabernacle, thus explaining the origin of the *Ner Tamid,* the Eternal Light.

The Midrash not only explains and links together events found in the Torah, especially those that are difficult to understand, but it completes unfinished stories.

Consider, for example, the legend of Serah bat Asher. In the Bible the name Serah is mentioned only twice. She is listed among those who went down into Egypt (Gen. 46:17) with Jacob and among those counted in the census that Moses took in the wilderness (Num. 26:46) about three hundred years later! The rabbis assumed that the Serah bat Asher in the first list was the same as the one in the second. How could she have lived for three centuries or more? The rabbis attributed her long life to a good deed that she had performed. When the sons of Jacob had just returned from Egypt after discovering that Joseph was alive, they were afraid to tell their father, fearing that he might not be able to withstand the shock. So they asked young Serah to find a way to break the news gently. Serah, who often played for Jacob, sang a little song, gently repeating that Joseph was alive. At first, Jacob did not understand, but, when the words sank in, he was overjoyed and gave Serah a blessing of long life.

As with most of the characters in the Midrash, once they appeared on the scene they were too good to ignore. And so it is with Serah, who lived through the entire period from Joseph to Moses, watching the Israelites fall from their position as an honored people into slavery and experiencing the Exodus from Egypt as well.

Serah was no idle bystander; she played an active role in the midrashic retelling of the Exodus. Just before the Israelites departed from Egypt, Moses went in search of Joseph's coffin. According to the story, Moses searched everywhere for the coffin, but no one knew its whereabouts. Then he met Serah, who told him she knew the place because she had been alive when Joseph was buried. Serah then led Moses to the site on the shore of the Nile and pointed to a spot in the river. Moses stood there and called out, "Joseph, Joseph, the time has come. If you want to come with us, come now." At that moment the golden coffin of Joseph floated like a feather to the surface.

The story of Serah bat Asher does not end there. An episode in the Talmud recounts that Rabbi Yohanan asked his students what the walls of the Red Sea had looked like while the sea was parted for the Israelites to cross. He then answered his own question: They looked like sprouting bushes. Suddenly a voice from outside the house of study was heard: "No, it wasn't like that at all! They looked like reflecting mirrors!" Startled, Rabbi Yohanan looked up and saw a little old woman leaning against the window. When he asked her who she was, she identified herself as Serah bat Asher!

One legend holds that Serah lived until the twelfth century, when she died in a fire in a synagogue in Isfahan, Persia. Her tomb, inscribed with the date 1133 C.E., became a holy pilgrimage site for the Jews of Iran. Still another legend holds that Serah never died—that she was taken up into Paradise alive, avoiding the taste of death.

In this book, Mrs. Freehof retells legends from the Talmud and the Midrash, which go back more than 1,500 years. They resolve mysteries about key biblical figures—how the serpent deceived Eve into tasting the fruit, how Adam received a magic book that foretold the future, how Abraham overthrew King

Nimrod, with whom Jacob wrestled, and how Jacob learned that Joseph was still alive.

Mrs. Freehof's original *Bible Legend Book* consisted of three volumes. The stories in the first two volumes were based on the rabbinic legends linked to the Torah, especially to the books of Genesis and Exodus. The stories in this volume have been selected from her first volume and focus on such primary characters of the biblical narrative in Genesis as Adam and Eve, Noah, Abraham and Rebecca, Jacob, and Joseph.

All these tales address questions that are left unanswered in the Torah. The rabbis searched the text as if secrets were deliberately concealed. That is how the Midrash works. That is what *drash,* the root word of "midrash," means: "to search" or "to discover." In reading between the lines, the rabbis discovered the answers they sought and in the process created a body of beautiful literature.

The great scholar Louis Ginzberg was one of the first to collect and publish these legends. In his seven-volume masterpiece, *The Legends of the Jews,* Ginzberg combined thousands of legends from a multitude of sources to create a book that follows all the biblical events, but through the prism of the rabbis.

Mrs. Freehof, recognizing the greatness of Ginzberg's accomplishment, was the first to adapt this literature for young readers so they too could marvel at the richness of our tradition and enjoy the stories that have been handed down from generation to generation.

Howard Schwartz

❦ 1 ❦

The Moaning of the Winds

It is recounted in Genesis that the creation of Adam and Eve was preceded by five days in which the rest of the world was brought into being. On the first day God created the heaven and the earth and separated darkness and light. On the second day the waters above were separated from those below. On the third day the waters on earth were gathered together so that dry land appeared, and trees and plants of every kind blossomed forth. On the fourth day the sun and moon and stars were created. On the fifth day all various creatures that creep and all winged birds were created. On the sixth day all the rest of the Creation was completed, including wild beasts and cattle and Adam, the first man. Sometime after this, God put Adam to sleep and withdrew one of his ribs, from which he created Eve. Adam and Eve were placed in a beautiful and fruitful garden, the Garden of Eden, where the only prohibition God gave them was not to eat the fruit of the Tree of Knowledge of Good and Evil.

One day, long ago, there gathered on the highest mountain of the earth, the North Wind, the South Wind, the West Wind, and the East Wind. There, on the summit, as quietly as a whisper, each wind breathed and moaned as if in sorrow.

1

The Peak of the Mountain heard the moaning of the winds and said, "O North Wind, why do you sigh so sadly?"

"Strong and friendly Mountain," said the North Wind, "you stand above the earth so high, with your gaze toward heaven. You cannot see the trouble in the world at your feet."

"Yes, O Mountain," said the West Wind, "we who blow all around the world, we winds know that today something sad has happened on earth."

"Today is only the sixth day of Creation," said the South Wind, "yet everything in the universe is weeping."

"Even God who created the world," the East Wind added, "is sad at what is happening."

"I knew that something dreadful was going on," said the Peak of the Mountain. "I saw the Sun grow dark and heard the Clouds weep, but I do not know why. Please tell me what terrible thing can have happened."

"Listen, O Mountain," the North Wind said, "and we shall tell you the story of Adam and Eve.

"You, O Mountain, who cannot move, have never seen the wonderful garden which God has made. It is the most beautiful place in all the world."

The grass there is bright green and like a thick, velvet carpet. The roses are large and red and so fragrant that their scent perfumes the whole garden. The birds sing more sweetly than anywhere else on earth. All the animals are friends. Everyone is kind. And, into this marvelous garden, Death has never come. There is only light and music, pleasure and life.

And then, in this paradise, God placed Adam. The man towered above all the creatures. So tall was he that, while his feet were on the ground, his head reached into the sky; and so broad was he that his body spread from east to west. And he was as handsome as he was powerful. But more remarkable than his strength and his grace was his character. He was honest. He was good. He was noble.

"Everything in this garden is yours, Adam," God said. "You

may use it as you wish. But there is one thing which I forbid. You must never eat the figs of the fig tree."

"I promise," answered Adam.

After a few happy hours had passed, Adam began to feel lonely. So God made Eve out of Adam's rib, and she became his wife. He explained to her immediately that she could have everything in the garden she wanted, except the figs from the fig tree. He warned her that it was forbidden fruit, that she must never touch it; and she promised.

After a while she wandered around by herself to see all the wonders of the garden. She admired whatever she saw. And every moment brought her a new delight. As she walked along enjoying the loveliness of Eden, she met the Serpent.

He was a very clever fellow. When he wished, he could walk upright. He could speak like a man. And he was jealous because God had made man master of the animals. He thought that he was just as good as Adam, if not better. So he cunningly plotted to bring about Adam's downfall. As he walked along, brooding over his resentment, making his plans, he met Eve.

"Oh, hello, Eve," said the Serpent.

"Hello, Serpent," said Eve.

"You are very beautiful, Eve."

"Oh, thank you." She was pleased with the compliment.

"I wonder why," said the Serpent slyly, "a woman as beautiful as you should be so stupid."

"I am not stupid," she protested.

"If you aren't stupid," the Serpent said, "then why do you let Adam tell you what you may or may not do? Just look at this fig tree." He put his hand out and touched it. "See what luscious fruit grows on the tree." He plucked a big yellow fig off a branch. "And Adam won't even permit you to touch the tree upon which this grows."

"It isn't Adam who forbids it, but God," Eve said.

"Don't you know why?" the Serpent asked. "The fig tree is

the Tree of Knowledge. If you eat its fruit, you will know as much as God. At present you and Adam are the masters of earthly creation. But, if you don't hurry and eat a fig from the Tree of Knowledge and become independent, God will soon make other creatures who will rule over you."

"I most certainly would not like that," Eve said. "I want to be queen of everything and every creature." She began to extend her hand towards the tree, then quickly she pulled it back. "But," she whispered, "if I eat the fig, I will die!"

"That's nonsense," said the Serpent. "Look." He took a big, juicy bite out of the fig which he held. "Look, Eve. I have eaten it, and I am not dead. Nor will you die if you eat it."

Then Eve said to herself, "The Serprent is eating the fig and no harm is coming to him; Adam is foolish not to eat it, too; right now I am better than the Serpent, but, if he eats the fig and I do not, he will soon be *my* superior; oh, I'd better hurry!"

"I will eat a fig," she said to the Serpent. "Get one down for me."

The Serpent quickly reached up into the leaves and took a big, ripe fig off the branch. Eve took it from him and was about to sink her teeth into it.

But again she hesitated. "I will not bite into it. Maybe I shouldn't eat the fruit itself. I will be careful. First I shall eat only a bit of the skin."

So she scraped the skin with her front teeth and ate it. Then she held the fig out at arm's length, waiting to see what would happen.

"Look," Eve said to the Serpent. "Look, I ate a piece of the skin. I didn't fall to the ground. I didn't die. Nothing happened!"

"Didn't I tell you that it was perfectly safe?" asked the Serpent.

"You are right," Eve said. "Nothing can happen to me if I eat the fruit, too."

And so Eve ate the whole fig. Then immediately, she became frightened.

"Oh, Serpent," she cried. "Now I am afraid. Oh, you were wicked to persuade me to eat it. My husband will be angry. Oh, I am really frightened."

Then she thought that, if she could coax Adam into eating a fig, perhaps he would share her guilt. "If I am going to be punished for my disobedience," she said to herself, "I do not want to suffer alone."

So she took one of the figs to Adam. And he, not stopping to realize what she was giving him, ate the fig. But the moment he tasted it, he knew that he had committed a sin, and he cried, "Oh! Why did you give me a fig from that tree! You have made me disobey God!"

That was the story which the winds told the Peak of the Mountain.

"Oh! It is a sad story!" exclaimed the Peak. "Then surely God must have punished Adam and his wife."

"Yes, indeed," said the North Wind. "But, before we tell you what happened to them, you will want to know who else was punished."

"Who else?" asked the Peak. "Only Adam and Eve were the guilty ones, weren't they? Why should anyone else suffer?"

"The sin of the Serpent was worse than that of Adam and Eve," the South Wind said. "Even though God had forbidden Adam and Eve to eat the fig, it was the Serpent who tricked them into doing wrong. And God said that one who persuades someone else to be wicked does more harm than the one who commits the sin."

"I can understand that," said the Peak of the Mountain. "How was the Serpent punished?"

"His power of speech was taken away. He never spoke another word," said the North Wind. "And his hands and feet disappeared. Now he must crawl through the mud and eat only dust. And, from now on, the Serpent and human beings will be enemies."

"So was the Serpent punished," said the East Wind. "And the surface of the earth was guilty, too."

And the South Wind explained, "You see, O Mountain, the Sun and the Earth had been appointed to be witnesses to testify against Adam should he break his promise. When he did, the Sun covered his face, and the world grew dark. But the Earth, not knowing what to do, did nothing at all. And God said that was cowardly."

"But what could the Earth have done?" asked the Peak.

"She could have groaned," said the East Wind.

"She could have rumbled," said the West Wind.

"She could have quaked," said the North Wind.

Then the South Wind said, "The Moon, too, was punished."

"The Moon!" cried the Peak of the Mountain. "Why, the Moon is a friend of mine. I speak to her every night as she moves among the stars. Oh, tell me, why was my friend, the beautiful Moon, punished?"

"When Adam and Eve broke their promise," the North Wind explained, "everything in the universe wept with them. We winds howled, and the Sun wept, and the Stars, and all the Angels shed bitter tears. The Sea stormed, and the Clouds cried. And even God had pity for Adam and Eve. But, the Moon *laughed*."

"Oh, that was unkind," said the Peak of the Mountain.

"It was more than unkind," sighed the East Wind. "It showed that the Moon had no mercy. So God had to punish her, too, by forcing her to grow old each month, to die and to have to be reborn anew."

"From now on, O Mountain," said the South Wind, "you will not see the Moon always full and bright as in the past. In the future, you will see first a quarter-moon at the beginning of the month, then a half-moon, then a three-quarter moon. Only for a day or two at the end of the month will you see the full moon in all her splendor and glory."

"Now," whistled the North Wind, "now we will tell you what happened to Adam and Eve."

At the very moment that Adam ate the forbidden fruit, he felt his whole body drawing and pulling together. His legs pulled up and his arms pulled in, his neck pulled down and his shoulders drew together.

"I feel so strange," cried Adam. "Something is happening to my body. I feel everything drawing and pulling."

And still his body pulled. His legs pulled up and his arms pulled in, his neck pulled down and his shoulders drew together. And Adam looked at his legs, then at his arms, then at his knees, and he touched his shoulders.

"Oh," he cried, "I am growing smaller. I used to be so big and tall. My head reached into the skies. And now, look how my body has shrunk. See how short I have become. My head does not even touch the treetops. Oh, what has happened to me?"

And the Serpent laughed and laughed. "Your wonderful big stature has shriveled, Adam." And again the Serpent laughed. "You used to be the tallest creature in the world. Now you are only of average size."

"Oh," cried Adam, "this must be God's punishment for my having eaten the fig."

While Adam was shrinking from his great size, something else was happening. To avoid seeing Adam's disgrace, the Sun covered his face, causing the world to grow dark.

The sudden darkness frightened Adam. "Look how black the world has become. My great height has shrunk, and now the world is dark. All because I ate that fig!" Then he turned to Eve and said, "O foolish woman, why did you give me a fruit from the forbidden tree?"

Eve was frightened, too, and ready to cry. "Let's hide among the trees," she whispered, "so God can't find us."

"Do you think you can hide from God?" Adam said. "God can see everywhere, no matter where you hide. But I know you are afraid to be alone, and I will go with you. Before I ate the fig I could not have walked beneath the branches. I was too tall. But now, for my sin, I am made small. Come, let us find shelter beneath the trees."

Then, when Adam and Eve heard the sound of God approaching the Garden of Eden, they were afraid, and they ran and crouched beneath the trees.

God stood at the gate of the garden. "Tell Me, Adam, where are you?"

From among the trees where he was hidden, Adam answered, "I heard Your voice in the garden, and I was afraid."

"Never before were you afraid of My voice, Adam. You have heard it often. You have sinned, Adam. You have disobeyed Me. That is why now you fear Me."

Now God wanted to give Adam a chance to repent for his wrongdoing. If he had only said he was sorry, God would have forgiven him at once. But Adam was stubborn. Besides, he was afraid to take the blame for what he had done. So, instead of saying, "I am sorry, I repent my sins," he tried to prove his innocence and said, "It wasn't my fault. As long as I lived alone, I did not sin. It was my wife's fault. She tempted me."

And God said, "Now you are committing two more sins. Besides being disobedient to Me, you are disloyal to her and ungrateful to Me. I did not give you a wife until you asked for one. I gave her to you to be a helpmate. You should have taken the responsibility, and you should have said to your wife, 'No, we will *not* disobey God.'"

But still, neither Adam nor Eve admitted that they were sorry for what they had done.

So God had to punish them because they were stubborn and would not confess their mistake. He banished them forever from the wondrous Garden of Eden.

"And that is the story," the North Wind said, "of how Adam and Eve were turned out of Paradise."

"Come," said the South Wind. "It is time for us to blow to our own corners. Come, we have tarried too long."

"Good-bye, Mountain," whistled the winds.

"Good-bye," cried the Peak of the Mountain.

And the four winds blew to the north, the south, the east, and the west.

Commentary

Of every tree of the garden you are free to eat; but as for the tree of knowledge of good and bad, you must not eat of it; for as soon as you eat of it, you shall die.   Genesis 2:16–17

*   *   *

In this story the Tree of Knowledge is identified as a fig tree. The biblical account does not name the tree (its identification with the apple came much later), resulting in much debate among the rabbis, who variously identified the fruit as grapes, wheat (which is not a fruit), the *etrog* (a part of the ritual of *Sukot*), and the fig. (*Berachot* 40a) The fig was thought to be the fruit because, after eating the forbidden fruit, Adam and Eve wrapped themselves in the leaves of the fig tree: *And they sewed together fig leaves and made themselves loincloths.* (Gen. 3:7)

*   *   *

Who deserves the blame for the Fall? Is it Adam, Eve, or the serpent? Rabbinic legends are remarkably consistent in going as far as possible to forgive Adam and Eve—who are, after all, the father and mother of the human race—and absolve them from blame. Adam is portrayed as wishing to share the fate of his wife, no matter what this might involve. According to this legend, Eve came to him after she had already eaten the fruit, in a state of fear, and Adam agreed to eat the fruit out of love for her. The Midrash goes to great lengths to show how reluctant Eve was to eat the fruit, first tasting the skin and only then, when nothing happened, eating the whole fruit. The one who gets the blame from the rabbinic perspective is, of course, the serpent. It was the serpent, after all, who convinced Eve to eat the fruit. According to the Midrash, the serpent pushed Eve against the trunk of the Tree of Knowledge to prove to Eve that it wasn't dangerous. This legend grows out of the difference between what God forbids Adam to do (eat the fruit of the Tree of Knowledge) and what Eve tells the serpent God has forbidden them to do (eat or even touch the fruit). The clever serpent notices the distinction and uses it as a means of convincing Eve to eat the fruit. Since God's warning against eating the fruit was made even before Eve was created, Eve learned of it from Adam, who likely told her not to eat or even touch the fruit of the tree. This exaggerated warning, it seems, later came back to haunt him. (*Genesis Rabbah* 19)

* * *

According to one midrash, Adam's shrinking from the size of a giant to the size of a mortal is one of the consequences of the Fall—the term used to describe the sin of Adam and Eve and their punishment. Others include the loss of the cloud of glory that was said to have surrounded Adam and Eve, the loss of a primordial light in which they could see from one end of the world to the other, and the suffering of various punishments as a result of their expulsion. (*Pirke de-Rabbi Eliezer* 14)

Write Your Own Midrash

There are many unsolved mysteries about the Fall of Adam and Eve that lend themselves to the writing of original midrashim. What was the nature of the Tree of Life in the Garden of Eden? Its role in the Genesis narrative is unclear. How did all of the birds and beasts in the Garden of Eden get their names? What happened to all of these birds and beasts once Adam and Eve left the garden? What became of the garments that God gave to Adam and Eve when they were cast out of the garden? These are just a few of the questions you might try to answer by writing a midrash of your own. The best method of doing this is to read some rabbinic legends on the subject, such as those found in Louis Ginzberg's *The Legends of the Jews* (or its one-volume version, *Legends of the Bible*). In addition many books of Midrash have been translated into English, including the *Midrash Rabbah, Pirke de-Rabbi Eliezer, Sefer Hayashar,* and *The Chronicles of Jerahmeel.* The Babylonian Talmud itself is a rich source. See the bibliography at the end of this book for a more complete listing. Once you have found the book, check its table of contents or index to find your subject. Then compare the biblical text with the versions presented in the Midrash. Perhaps one of these midrashic legends will lend itself to some kind of embellishment or retelling; perhaps you will find an issue in the biblical text that the rabbis have not resolved and make it the subject of your own midrash. Try to be true to the spirit of the Midrash but otherwise give your imagination wings.

✲2✲

The Wicked Brother

Having disobeyed God and eaten the fruit of the Tree of Knowledge, Adam and Eve were banished from the Garden of Eden. They were permitted to take with them only the garments of animal skin that God had made for them. Outside of Eden, their lives became a struggle for survival. Soon after their expulsion, Adam and Eve became parents. Their first child, Cain, is described in Genesis as a farmer ("a tiller of the soil"); their second, Abel, as a shepherd ("a keeper of sheep").

To live in Eden was to live in Paradise. There life was sweet and peaceful. There the animals were carefree and friendly. There food was plucked off every tree, and fresh water flowed in every stream.

To be driven from Eden was sad beyond words. Unhappy and lonely were Adam and Eve when the gates of the garden closed behind them, and they looked at the outside world.

"The world is so empty!" said Adam. "Where are the trees?"

"Where are the flowers?" asked his little son Cain.

"And where are the smiling streams?" asked Cain's brother Abel.

"I am worried," said Eve. "We shall starve. There is no food in the earth. It looks so brown and so sandy."

"Don't be afraid," Adam said. He also was worried, but he wanted to comfort his wife. "You and I are lucky, Eve. At least our lives were spared. Besides, we have Cain and Abel, our two sons."

"But what will we feed our children? There is no food."

Just then they heard a voice calling, "Adam! Adam!"

They all looked around and saw one of the archangels.

"I am Michael," said the angel, coming close to them. "I shall teach you how to find food."

"Where will we look for it?" asked Adam.

"Right here," Michael answered. "Here where you stand. This ground will give forth food. You will make it grow from the earth. See, here in my hand I have seeds for you to plant. These are the kernels of wheat and barley, these of peas and beans, and these of apple and cherry trees. Food will grow from all these seeds—food to still your hunger."

"You have cheered our hearts," said Adam. "Now we know that we will have food. Now we will not starve."

Michael nodded, smiling at Adam, glad to see him happy again. "I shall stay with you for three days and teach you how to be a farmer."

"Good! But tell me, Michael. How long must the seed lie in the ground until it becomes food that we can eat?"

"A harvest usually takes many months."

"Many months!" exclaimed Eve. "Oh, that's dreadful. We have only enough food to last us a few days!"

"Don't you worry, Eve," Michael said, smiling. "This will not be the usual harvest. As a special blessing, this first harvest will be ready in three days. But ever after, a harvest will take many months."

Michael stayed with Adam and Eve and their two sons, Cain and Abel, and he taught Adam and the boys how to plow the ground and till the soil, how to plant the seeds and pull up the weeds, and how to cut the wheat. After three days, the wonderful harvest was ripe. Adam and his sons gathered it in.

Michael taught them the farmer's final lesson, how to gather a completed crop. Then, satisfied that they could now earn their living from the soil, he bade them farewell and departed.

Adam and Eve never forgot the Garden of Eden, but, as the years passed, they were becoming content with life outside. They now had food, and they built a shelter. Their family life could have been happy were it not for what happened to their two sons.

Abel was friendly and generous. He was willing to play quietly and fairly with Cain, but Cain was a troublemaker. He was selfish and loud. He could never agree with Abel about anything. He wanted always to be the leader, to be master. And Abel, though he was quiet and easygoing, resented his older brother's lordly attitude. And so the boys frequently quarreled.

One day Eve said to her husband, "Oh, Adam, I am worried about our boys. I fear that some day Cain will harm or perhaps even slay Abel."

Adam laughed. "Why, Eve! Where did you get such a foolish notion? Do you really imagine that Cain is so cruel that he would slay his own brother?"

"My fears come from a dream," Eve said. "Last night I dreamed that Cain murdered Abel."

"What a dreadful dream!" Adam exclaimed. "It frightens me, too. Of course, it is only a dream, but we had better guard against its ever coming true. I shall separate the two boys. Call them. Tell them I wish to speak with them."

In a few moments Cain and Abel were standing in front of their father. He said to them, "My sons, you are growing up. Soon you will both be men. Now it is time for you each to have your own home and to earn your own living."

"I would like that, Father," said Abel.

"So would I," said Cain.

"Good. You, Cain, will now own all the land north of the big oak tree, and the land to the south of it will belong to Abel."

"Good. Mine is the north," said Cain.

"And mine is the south," said Abel.

"Cain," said Adam, "you shall be a farmer. You will till the soil. Abel, you shall be a shepherd. You will keep the flocks of sheep."

Adam's plan for keeping the two boys apart worked well for a long time. The years passed, with Cain farming his land and Abel tending his flocks. But Cain never forgot his jealousy of his brother Abel.

One day Adam called his two sons to him and said, "My sons, in the month of Nisan, on the fourteenth day, you each must bring a sacrifice to God."

"What is a sacrifice, Father?" asked Abel.

"It is a gift that you bring to God. It must be something that you value. If you don't really want it for yourself, then it isn't a true gift."

"Do you mean, Father," asked Abel, "that if I have three sheep I should give them to God as a gift? Then I would have nothing left."

"You may keep two. But you must give up the best one of the three."

"Why the best?" asked Cain. "Why not the worst?"

"You must give the best you have because a true gift is the one *you* want to keep."

"I don't want to give away my best barley," said Cain, "and my best grapes. I grew them myself. They belong to me, and I won't give them to anybody else."

"No! They do *not* belong to you," said Adam. "Everything in the world belongs to God who only lends you the ground to grow food in and the rain to water your seeds and quench the dry earth. But all of it really belongs to God. We bring God our sacrifice to show that we are grateful for our use of God's ground and seeds and rain."

"Well, I won't do it," said Cain. "Why should I work from early morning until late at night just to give God a present?"

"That is selfish and stubborn talk. I do not like it," Adam said. "Now listen to me, my sons. Tomorrow we will build an altar. And, at sunrise on the fourteenth day of Nisan, you will bring your sacrifices to this altar. That is God's command, and we must obey."

The two young men left their father's house and walked away to their own dwellings. All the way Cain kept grumbling at this new foolishness. He was a grown man. He didn't have to do everything his father told him to do. Abel said nothing.

Very early on the fourteenth day of Nisan, just before the sun rose in the east, Abel got out of bed and dressed himself in his best clothes. He then went to his pasture and selected the finest sheep of his flock. Leading the sheep, he walked happily along the road in the cool air of the morning until he reached the altar. He put the sheep on it and said, "O God, with joy in my heart I bring You my gift."

In the next instant, a flame of heavenly fire consumed the sheep. And Abel, knowing that his gift had been accepted and blessed, sang for joy.

Meanwhile, Cain was still at home. When he saw the sun begin to rise, he got up and put on his oldest clothes, the ones he wore when he did his farm work. Then he cooked his breakfast, a big and hearty meal. He ate everything up to the last crumb. When he finished, he looked in the bin. All he could find were a few grains of flaxseed.

"These are good enough for the sacrifice," he muttered.

He took the few grains and wrapped them in a piece of dirty cloth. Then he sauntered along to the altar and threw the rag with the few grains of flaxseed upon it.

"There," said Cain. "There's my gift to God. It's good enough."

He waited. But his gift remained lying there. A few moments later a big eagle swooped down and snatched up the dirty cloth. As the huge bird flew away with it, the seed was scattered over the ground.

Cain flew into a rage. He shook his fist at the heavens. "Is that the way God treats my gift?" he shouted.

God called down, "O Cain, I shall not forgive you until you change your stubborn, selfish ways. Wickedness dwells in your heart. Drive it out. If you do not, evil will become your master and rule over you all your life."

But Cain pretended not to hear. Instead he rushed to Abel's house and began to quarrel with him.

"Why did God take your gift and not mine? I am as good as you are. But I see now that it doesn't matter whether I am good or evil."

And Abel answered him, "Why should God accept your miserable gift? Do you call a few grains wrapped in a dirty cloth a proper gift to present to our Creator? Your actions showed plainly that you have no respect. Then why should God respect you? Indeed, Cain, your selfishness and jealousy have blinded you."

Cain was too angry to answer. Without a word he turned away and rushed home, hating his brother more than ever.

"How I hate that brother of mine," Cain growled as he stepped into his own house. "He thinks he is so noble. I shall find a way of getting rid of him. Some day I will slay him."

One day while Cain was hoeing his cornpatch, one of Abel's sheep broke away from the flock and blundered onto Cain's farm and into his cornpatch, trampling it down. Cain flew into such a rage that he rushed to his brother and shouted at him, "I will kill you for that!"

"Be calm, Brother," Abel said. "I'm sorry about that sheep. You know it was only an accident."

But, instead of controlling his anger, Cain threw himself upon Abel and began to fight with him. And Abel fought back. They struck each other in the face. They gripped each other and began to wrestle. Abel was so much stronger than Cain that he threw him to the ground and held him down so that he could not move.

"Have pity, dear Abel," cried Cain. "You are too strong for me. You will kill me."

"I don't want to hurt you," Abel said. "I only want to keep you from killing me."

Cain was gasping for breath. "Oh, Abel, have mercy. I am helpless. If you will let me up from the ground, I will promise never to harm you again."

Abel believed Cain and released him. But, the moment he was free, Cain killed Abel.

Instantly, it grew dark, lightning flashed across the horizon, thunder roared in the sky, the winds shrieked, and the whole earth trembled. This was the first murder that the earth had seen.

Cain, shocked out of his anger and badly frightened, cried out, "Oh, what have I done? And what shall I tell my parents when they ask me where my brother is? They will soon know that I have killed him. I shall have to run away from here."

As he finished speaking, the earth stopped its trembling, the wind's howling died away to a moan, the lightning flashes faded away, the thunder moved on into the distance. But still it remained dark. Then, in that dusk, a large radiant light appeared. From the light spoke the voice of God.

"Wherever you run, O Cain, I will find you, in the darkest cave or on the highest mountain or in the deepest forest. Now answer Me, Cain. Where is your brother Abel?"

"How should I know?" Cain answered. "Am I my brother's keeper?"

"Yes. You are. People should protect other people. If people are in trouble, you should help them. If they are in pain, you should ease their suffering. If they are hungry, you should feed them."

Cain said insolently, "Oh, well. Abel is dead. What does it matter, anyway?"

"You murderer! It matters more than anything on earth. Every human being is precious. Life is the greatest gift in the world.

Every child that is born is a child of Mine. Do you think that I give life to the world only that the wicked like you may destroy it? You have committed the greatest sin that anyone can commit. And for that sin you shall have your punishment. From this day on you will be a wanderer over the face of the earth. No spot in the world will let you rest on it. The wild beasts will seek to devour you. The tame animals will fear you, and no human being will ever speak to you again."

Terror seized hold of Cain, and he cried, "Where can I hide? Where can I escape this fearful punishment?"

"You may flee from your parents; you can never escape from Me. Into your heart have I implanted fear. Know that all creation will hate the name of Cain, the name of a murderer. The earth will scorn you, and the sun and the moon and the stars. You will be despised."

The voice of God ceased. The radiance faded. Cain was left alone in the darkness.

From that day Cain became a wanderer over the face of the world. All living things turned away from him. All nature scorned him. If he tried to farm the ground, thorns and thistles grew instead of corn and wheat. If he tried to rest his head on a stone, it bruised him. And, worst of all, by day and by night his bitter thoughts gave him no rest. Wherever he wandered, in the valleys or on the mountains, in the desert or in the meadow, in his own heart he heard the terrifying words, "Cain, you have slain your brother."

Commentary

The Lord said to Cain, "Where is your brother Abel?" And he said, "I do not know. Am I my brother's keeper?"　　　　Genesis 4:9

*　　*　　*

Eve's dream that Cain would slay Abel is an example of a prophetic dream. Such dreams are often found in rabbinic literature for the rabbis believed that in dreams God revealed to humans secrets about the future.

*   *   *

This story attributes Cain's rage at Abel to the rejection of Cain's offering to God. The Midrash holds that this offering was not of the finest quality nor was it given in the proper spirit. (*Genesis Rabbah* 22:5–6) This reading closely follows the biblical text, in which the murder takes place immediately after Cain's offering is refused. However, other motives for the murder are found in the Talmud and Midrash. One explanation is that Cain and Abel argued over their possessions, with Cain possessing all the land and Abel all creeping things. Cain ordered Abel off the land (since Cain owned all of the land, where else was Abel to go?), and Abel told Cain to remove his garment, which was woven from the wool of Abel's flocks. (*Pirke de-Rabbi Eliezer* 21) Another explanation was that Cain and Abel were each born with a twin sister. Cain desired Abel's twin, who was the most beautiful, and said, "I will slay Abel my brother, and I will take his twin sister from him." (*Pirke de-Rabbi Eliezer* 21) One of the most fascinating aspects of these legends is that all these contradictory explanations were allowed to stand and were repeated from generation to generation. This practice demonstrates that Judaism allows for multiple interpretations of both law and legend.

*   *   *

In our version of the tale of Cain, his fate is left unresolved, as it is in the Torah. But the rabbis were fascinated with the question of how Cain was ultimately punished for committing the first murder on earth. In fact, four versions of Cain's death appear in rabbinic sources. In one of these Cain is said to have died in the Flood. This, however, was not regarded as a satisfactory punishment since it did not single out Cain for his crime. In another version Cain is transformed into the Angel of Death—

an appropriate punishment for the first murderer. (*Midrash Tanchuma Berachot* 11) In yet another, Cain was killed when the stones of his house collapsed on him. Thus, in a way, he was stoned, the punishment for murder. (*Book of Jubilees* 4:31) But the version that became most popular has Cain slain by his own descendant, Lamech. Cain was still wandering the earth generations after the murder. Lamech, once a great hunter, had in old age become blind, requiring the help of his son Tubal-cain (whose name shows he has descended from Cain). Tubal-cain would sight an animal and guide his father in the right direction; Lamech would then shoot his arrow. One day the boy sighted a horn in a thicket and pointed Lamech toward it. When they went to see what Lamech had killed, they discovered the body of Cain. (*Sefer Hayashar* 2)

Write Your Own Midrash

There are many unresolved questions about Cain and Abel. First, if they were alone in the world, whom did they marry? What did they fight over? What happened to Cain in the end? These questions were addressed by the rabbis in the Midrash. Other answers are possible, of course, and you might try your hand at these or other questions that arouse your curiosity.

✤ 3 ✤

The Blue Sapphire Book

The generations following Adam and Eve became increasingly evil. The reason, perhaps, is linked to a midrash which expounds upon the legend found in Genesis 6, describing how the divine beings, the "sons of God" (which the rabbis interpreted to mean angels) took wives from among the daughters of mortals. Their offspring, giants called Nephilim, taught people all kinds of evil, including how to make weapons and wage war on each other. The evil ways of humans greatly concerned God who finally concluded that it was necessary to blot out the world in a great flood, *"for I regret that I made them."* (Gen. 6:7) Of all the people on the earth, only one man, Noah, and his family found God's favor.

Once there lived a man named Methuselah who went on a very strange journey. He left his house and walked until he approached the farthest mountains, then on he went until he reached the distant horizon, then further and further until he came to the end of the earth. On the very rim of the world he stood still and cried aloud, "Enoch! O my father Enoch!"

On the wings of the echo came back a murmur, "This is the voice of Enoch. Is it my son Methuselah whom I hear?" Then Enoch himself appeared on the edge of the world.

24

"O Father, it is I, your son."

"Why do you call me away from the place on high where now I am one with the heavenly hosts? Has something gone wrong in the world below?"

"Yes. Something strange has occurred this very day. To my son Lamech a child has just been born who is more like an angel than a child of a mortal. His hair is long and thick as wool, his body is white as fresh-fallen snow, his eyes are like the brilliant rays of the sun, and his face is as radiant as an angel's."

"I already know of the birth of this wonderful boy," said Enoch. "This is the child who will, one day, save the world, for the world is in danger of destruction. The people of the earth are wicked. They cheat. They lie. They steal. If they continue their evil practices, God will send a great flood to destroy them."

"A flood? But, Father, a flood would destroy the good people of the earth, too," protested Methuselah.

"No, my son. The good people will be saved by your little grandson, whose name will be Noah. God will teach him how to protect all good people and all good creatures from the flood."

"If that flood must come, then at least my grandson will be safe."

"Now," said Enoch, "I shall tell you why your grandson was chosen for this great task of rescuing the good people. Do you remember my great adventure, when, during my lifetime, I went up into heaven to be shown all the wonders of the universe?"

"Yes. I remember hearing you tell of it many times."

"At that time, God told me that He would send His two angels, Ariuk and Mariuk, to guard over my descendants, to protect them from being drowned in this flood. And God has selected my great-grandson Noah to save from destruction those who worship God. So I had known of this long ago. Now you know it, too. Now go home. Tell your son Lamech to train his son that he may be worthy of the task that awaits him. And now, farewell, my son."

"Farewell, my father."

Enoch vanished into a large white cloud, and Methuselah was left standing alone on the rim of the world. He turned away and walked back until he reached the distant horizon. Then on he went until he approached the farthest mountains, then further and further until he came, at last, to his own country. Finally, after having traveled for many days, Methuselah arrived at his own home.

There he found his son, Lamech, the father of little Noah, waiting for him. Methuselah told the story of his conversation with Enoch, and together they planned how best to raise their unusual child.

Noah had a happy childhood. Although he grew up just like other children, he had certain special talents. He was inventive. He made the tools for farming—the first plow, the first scythe, and the first hoe—which turned agriculture from a burden into a pleasant occupation.

He married and had three sons whose names were Shem, Ham, and Japheth whom he guided in the righteous paths of their ancestors. They became worthy descendants of Methuselah and Enoch.

One morning Noah walked out into his garden. The moment he left the shelter of his house, the brightness of the day struck him as being unusual. The sun shone with its usual light, but one corner of the garden, near the row of poplar trees, glittered and blazed so much that it hurt his eyes. What makes my garden so strangely bright, he wondered, as he strode quickly over to a long, narrow bench at which he liked to sit and think and study every morning and evening.

There, on the bench, was an object he had never seen before. It was a book—but no ordinary book. It was made of bright blue sapphires!

"A Blue Sapphire Book!" said Noah to himself. "It's the most marvelous book I have ever seen. No earthly hand has made it. How does it come in my garden? To whom does it belong?"

He rubbed his hands along the sides of his robe to make

sure they were clean. Then, carefully, he stooped over and took one corner between his fingers and raised the cover of the book.

Across the top of the first page, large and bold letters proclaimed: **This is the Book of God!**

"Oh!" Noah staggered back, letting the cover drop. He looked at his fingertips. They felt cold, yet tingled from having touched the precious stones. "A Book of God! How does such a book come to be on my bench?" He looked up at the sun. "The sun is very hot today. Perhaps I have had a sunstroke, and I imagine I see a book that does not really exist." So he turned his back on the book, covered his eyes to rest them, and counted to fifty. Then, opening his eyes again, taking a deep breath, he turned slowly. And he saw that the Blue Sapphire Book was still there. He touched it gently.

"I am not dreaming," he murmured. "It does exist." Then, feeling bolder, he opened it again, turned the first page, and read it.

> To Noah, the grandson of Methuselah, the great-grandson of Enoch, has this book been sent. Read the words written here, O Noah. Pay attention to them, and all will go well with you and yours.

A great excitement took hold of Noah so that he trembled violently. But on he read of how the wicked people have greatly angered God. They do only evil and must be destroyed. To rid the earth of them, God will send a flood which will cover the earth for a whole year.

"A flood!" Noah exclaimed. "A flood will destroy everything. Oh, must I and my wife and my sons perish? Let me read on!" He turned back to the book.

> Everyone and everything on earth will drown in this flood except the family of Noah.

"Except my family? But how can we be saved when the disaster will be worldwide?" He read on.

To Noah and his sons is given the task of building an ark. It will be a house on a ship. It will float safely over the waters for many months until the earth is dry again. When the flood comes, Noah will take his family and all the good animals of the earth into the ark. There they will be safe from harm.

Noah read on and on, through every page of the book, until he came to the very end. Then he sighed and gently closed the book. With great care he picked it up, held it close to him, and carried it into his house. At once the whole room was lighted as if with a thousand candles. On the table he put a square of purple velvet, and there he placed the Blue Sapphire Book.

Quietly and calmly, he called his sons to him. Shem, Ham, and Japheth all exclaimed in wonder when they saw the book. What was it? Whose was it? Where did their father find it?

"My sons, a great honor and a great responsibility have been bestowed upon us." Then he told them the story of the heaven-sent book and the message it contained.

"How will we build this ark?" asked Shem. "And how big shall it be?"

"All that is carefully described in the book," answered Noah. "From the wood of the gopher tree it shall be made. It shall be thirty cubits in height, its width fifty, its length one hundred." Then he took a strongbox with bronze handles and a bronze lock, and into it he placed the Blue Sapphire Book. "Now come, my sons. Get your axes. Sharpen them. We will go into the woods and cut down the trees."

His sons obeyed without further question. Then, each carrying his ax over his shoulder, they and their father walked on down the road towards the woods. Soon they met a group of the wicked people.

"Ho, here is our friend, Noah," said the man who made idols.

"Accompanied by his three sons," added the man who worshiped idols.

"Look, they carry axes," cried the man who cursed God.

Noah and his sons did not answer the jibes of the wicked men. They just kept on walking.

"I suppose you are going to work in the forest," said the man who was cruel.

There was no answer.

"Tell me, O Noah," said the Murderer, "why do you work so hard?"

"Yes, tell us why," said the Cheater. "A single harvest of our rich ground is sufficient for forty years. So why work at all? You should be gay and merry and laugh the hours away."

"The gods we make of wood and jewels and precious stones are easy to worship," said the Blasphemer. "Why do you worship the unseen God who makes you work all the time?"

"Stop!" Noah commanded his sons. They all stood still and swung their axes to the ground. Noah turned to the wicked men—the Murderer, the Cheater, and the Blasphemer—and he said, "This is my answer to you. If we do not work, we become lazy, and lazy people cannot truly serve God."

"Oh, all that's nonsense," said the Insolent. "Work is misery. Work is drudgery. Work is dull. The carefree life is the happy life."

"You only think you are happy," said Noah. "But, beware! Your wicked ways will yet destroy you."

"You may be a righteous man," said the Scorner. "But you never have any fun."

"What do you call fun?" asked Noah. "You think it's fun to scorn everything good. He (pointing to the thief), although he has plenty himself, thinks it's fun to steal food from poor people. He (pointing to the slanderer) thinks it's fun to spread lies that hurt his friends. Well, I have my enjoyment, too. I think it's fun to be kindly and just. You can lead a worthwhile life and still have pleasure." But the wicked ones laughed at him. Noah lifted his ax to his shoulder and turned to his sons. "Come, my sons," he said. "These wicked people won't listen to reason. Come, let us go."

So Noah and his sons continued on their way to the woods. The wicked people followed, poking fun at them, laughing as they went. All along the way more and more evil people joined the procession. The Deceitful came and the Gambler, the Haughty, the Informer, and the Rogue.

When they reached the woods, Noah and his sons followed a narrow forest aisle until they came to the grove of the gopher trees. They set to work and began to cut the trees, and the wicked men watched and jeered.

The trees were sturdy. The sun was hot. The axes blistered their hands. They grew weary. Finally, after they had cut down four trees, they stopped to rest. When Noah put down his ax, the Spendthrift said, "Why are you cutting down those trees?"

"With them I shall build an ark."

"An ark?" laughed the Ungrateful Man. "I never heard of one. What is it? Another one of your inventions?"

"It will be a house on a boat," answered Noah.

"Why should you build such a house?" asked the Impudent Man.

"Because God will send a flood to destroy all those who will not change their evil ways."

The wicked people laughed and laughed.

"What kind of a flood can your God send?" asked the Miser, laughing so he could hardly talk. "If your God sends a flood of fire, we shall know how to protect ourselves. We'll run away from it."

"Don't laugh," warned Noah. "It will be no flood of fire, but a mighty outpouring of waters from the heavens. Not one of you will be able to save himself unless you stop being wicked!"

"Just when do we have to stop?" laughed the Hard-Hearted. "Tell us when, O Noah."

"The flood will come when my grandfather Methuselah dies."

"Ho ho. That's a long way off," laughed the wicked people. "He's going to live a long time."

"Let's leave these fools alone," cried the Malicious Man. "Let them cut trees and build arks. Come, let us go and be merry."

So they went away with their foolish laughter sounding from afar. But Noah and his sons continued to chop down gopher trees. When, after many days, they had cut enough, they split and trimmed them. And then they began to build the ark.

They worked all during the soft and gentle spring, during the hot and sticky summer, during the crisp and dry autumn, during the cold and crackling winter. Still they were not finished.

They worked another spring, summer, autumn, and winter. And still the work was not yet done.

They worked yet another spring, another summer, and then, at the beginning of the third autumn, the ark was at last completed. Now Noah had to gather enough food to last for one whole year. He had to get meat for the lions, fish for the cats, straw for the oxen. He had to get a different kind of food for every kind of animal.

Besides, during these many months, Noah pleaded constantly with the wicked men, begging them to give up their evil ways so that they, too, could be protected from the flood. But the more he talked to them, the more they mocked. And the more they mocked, the more wicked they became.

One day, Noah called them all together. "Listen now, you wicked people. The day of your doom is near. Soon, as I have repeatedly warned you, God will send down on earth a powerful flood, and you will all perish. I told you once that the flood would come when Methuselah, my grandfather, died. Listen now and tremble! He has just died!"

Some of the wicked people stopped laughing. Instead they shivered.

"You have one more chance," said Noah. "God will wait seven days more. You have one week in which to repent your sins."

"Oh, Noah is a fool," the wicked people cried. "And his God is a fool. What harm do they think they can do to us?" And they laughed and laughed, leaving him to return to their sinful ways.

Noah knew they would not repent, but he had pleaded with

them as much as he could. There was nothing more he could do. He turned away and went to the ark because he still had the task of gathering the animals. As he came to the door he saw Shem hurrying to him.

"Father," Shem cried, "something strange is happening! Look, the sun has risen in the west! See, the water in the river is flowing up instead of down!"

"I have been waiting for that," Noah said calmly. "It is a special sign. In the Blue Sapphire Book I read that, during the last seven days before the flood waters come, all the laws of nature will be reversed. Everything will go backwards."

"And will the wicked turn back from their evil?" asked Shem.

"I fear that will not happen. Now listen to me, Shem. The final instructions contained in the book were these—that the animals are to come to the ark in pairs. I am to admit them only if they have partners, and each animal must lie down and wait at the entrance."

As though his words were a signal, all the animals began to crowd toward the ark. Noah stood at the entrance to be sure that the animals came in pairs and that at the entrance to the ark they first lay down on the ground.

First the birds came: the martin and the mockingbird, and many others, thirty-two different kinds of them. And all kinds of animals came: wild creatures and gentle house pets; the boar and the bear, the cat and the dog, and many others of their kind.

Seven days passed. Then came the day when the flood was to begin. All the animals were in the ark by now, together with Noah's wife and his sons, Shem, Ham, and Japheth, and their wives. He was just about to close the door when a peculiar creature came up to the ark.

"O Noah," it said in a squeaky voice. "Please let me come in."

"Who are you?"

"I am Falsehood."

"I cannot take you in. Only animals and creatures in pairs may come in. You are alone. You have no partner so you cannot enter."

"Wait, please," cried Falsehood. "Don't close the door yet. It will only take me a moment to find a companion."

Falsehood sped away, but in one moment he was back, leading another peculiar creature by the hand. As they came near the ark, they lay down on the ground.

"And who are you?" Noah asked Falsehood's companion.

"I am Misfortune."

Now Noah did not want to keep Falsehood and Misfortune alive in the world. He wanted troubles and lies to die in the flood. But he could not keep them out because they fulfilled the required conditions. So he had to admit them. When they were inside, he stood in the doorway, waiting for the flood to begin.

Suddenly he noticed that a great crowd of people had gathered in front of the ark. There were seven hundred thousand of them. They were the wicked people.

"Save me, Noah, have mercy," cried the Man without Pity.

"Anything I have is yours, but save me," cried the Miser.

"Oh, help me, help!" shrieked the Coward.

"Quiet!" Noah thundered. "Aren't you the ones who said, 'There is no God'? Haven't I begged you for years and years to give up your evil ways? And you laughed at me and would not listen. Now it is too late. You cannot be saved. Away, away, you wicked ones!"

Noah turned his back on them. He went into the ark and closed the door.

Then, as he had read in the Blue Sapphire Book, two stars were plucked from the Constellation of the Pleiades, causing such a tremendous hole in the sky that all the waters stored in the first heaven came tumbling down to earth.

The waters struck and splashed, swirled around in mighty currents, and rose higher and higher and roared and boomed, streaming down steadily for forty long days and nights. There was only water to be seen on the earth, covering everything—the ground, the trees, the mountains.

At the end of forty days the rains stopped, but the water level did not drop for many months. The Flood lasted for one whole year. Everything on earth was destroyed. But Noah and his family and the animals were safe and dry inside the ark.

Commentary

Enoch walked with God; then he was no more, for God took him.   Genesis 5:24

*   *   *

The rabbis loved to imagine that the patriarchs who lived before Moses had access to the Torah. The legend of the Book of Raziel expresses that view, as the book that the angel Raziel shows to Adam is readily identified with the Torah. This story initiates what is known as a chain legend, in which an object—here the book given to Adam by the angel Raziel—is passed down from one generation to the next. Such chain midrashim are also told about the garments of Adam and Eve, the glowing stone known as the *Tzohar,* and the staff of Moses. (For more on the *Tzohar* see the "Introduction.")

*   *   *

In the Torah there is a direct line from Adam to Enoch to Methuselah to Lamech to Noah. Enoch appears only once in the Bible, in a genealogy about which it says of everyone else, "then he died." In the case of Enoch it says, "[he] *walked with God; then he was no more, for God took him.*" (Gen. 5:24) Based solely on this phrase, a rich legendary tradition grew up around Enoch, which described how he was taken into Paradise in a chariot and was transformed into the angel Metatron. Who is

Metatron? He is none other than the heavenly scribe, the prince of the treasuries of heaven, the ruler and judge of the angels, and the attendant of the Throne of Glory. (*Enoch Three* or the *Hebrew Book of Enoch*) Quite a promotion for a character who appears only in one genealogical passage!

* * *

In "The Blue Sapphire Book" Noah is described as finding the book in one corner of his garden. Another tradition holds that the book was first given to Adam by the angel Raziel and passed down until it reached Noah. A third tradition describes how Enoch hid the book in a cave before his ascent into heaven, and later he appeared to his son, Methuselah, in a dream, telling him where it was hidden. In this way it came to Lamech, son of Methuselah and father of Noah, and thus to Noah, who took it with him on the ark. Nor does the legend end with Noah. The book was said to have been passed down from Abraham to Isaac to Jacob to Joseph and eventually to King Solomon, who kept it in the Temple. Thus it was one of the precious objects lost when the Temple was destroyed.

Write Your Own Midrash

Imagine that the Blue Sapphire Book was *not* destroyed when the Temple in Jerusalem was destroyed but was among the treasures saved by the prophet Jeremiah and hidden in a cave. What became of it? Who else in Jewish history had need of it or deserved to receive it? What kind of secrets did it reveal? Try to trace the history of the book from the time of the Temple to the present, passing it on to one deserving sage or rabbi in each generation.

❧4❧

The Rainbow

Noah, his family, and pairs of all the animals remained in the ark during the forty days and nights of the Flood. The waters rose so high that they covered all the land, even the mountains, destroying every living thing on earth. After one hundred and fifty days, the waters began to subside. Noah sent a raven to see if the land had reappeared, but the bird did not return to the ark. Then Noah sent a dove, which returned because it could not find a resting place. Seven days later Noah again sent out the dove, and this time it came back with an olive leaf in its beak. This indicated that land had finally reappeared.

There is a graceful bridge across the sky, an arching bow of many colors. It is red and green, yellow and blue. Whenever the sun comes out to shine while the rain is falling, this rainbow stretches across the cloudy sky. Its feet disappear into the earth, and its arching back reaches the clouds.

This rainbow was not created at the beginning of the world as were the sun and moon and stars. Not until after the great Flood was it made. This is how God came to fashion the rainbow:

When the dove reported to Noah that the flood waters were beginning to go down, it was still many weeks before the ground could be clearly seen. Then one day, as the earth was beginning to dry out, Noah said to everyone in the ark, "Listen to me, animals and creatures! The Flood is over. Now the waters have left the earth, and you may all leave the ark."

All the animals cheered and whistled for joy.

"At last!" yelled the moose.

"It's about time!" hooted the owl.

"Three cheers!" squeaked the bat.

"Oh, it will be so wonderful to get out of this crowded boat," said the grasshopper, who had worried that whole long year that he would be stepped on.

"I'll be glad to be on some solid ice instead of rocking in this hot, old boat," said the penguin.

Everyone was happy, eager to get out.

"Stop pushing there," said the falcon to the butterfly.

"Don't step on me," cried the monkey to the hippopotamus.

"Let me out," snapped the woodpecker.

So, pushing and squirming and squealing and shoving, the animals poured out of the ark. Then Noah's wife, Naamah, said to Noah, "The ark is empty. Everyone has gone. Now we too can go."

But Noah said, "No, I cannot go yet. I entered the ark because God told me to. I cannot leave it until God says I can."

God heard Noah's words and said, "Noah! Now you may leave the ark."

But Noah said, "O God, if You command me to leave, I shall leave, but I would rather remain here. If I go out into the world and settle on dry land again, someday You may send another flood, and I and my family shall surely be destroyed. O God, promise me, as I leave the safety of the ark, that You will never again send another flood on earth."

"Very well," God said. "You deserve to be happy because you were obedient. It was hard work building the ark, assembling the animals, and finding the food. But you obeyed. Therefore, now I shall reward you with the promise that never again shall I send a flood to cover the whole earth."

"Oh, thank You for that promise," cried Noah. "Now I am content to leave the ark."

Noah followed his wife and his sons, Shem, Ham, and Japheth, and their wives out of the ark. They came out onto the muddy land and, looking around in dismay, saw that the world was utterly ruined.

"There are no roads or bridges left," cried Japheth.

"Oh, look how every tree has rotted," exclaimed Ham.

"There is nothing growing in the ground," sighed Shem.

"There's not a single house left to live in," wept Naamah. "The whole world is in ruins!"

When Noah, looking slowly around at the world, saw the complete destruction, he said, "The earth is mud. The trees are sticks. The hills are barren stones." He turned to his sons. "We are the only people left on earth. We shall have to rebuild the whole world and make it fair and habitable again. Now come, my sons, I shall divide the earth among you, and each will rebuild his portion."

He took three flat pieces of stone. On one he wrote the word "north," on another "south," on the third "center." He put them in his bosom, and each son drew one out.

Shem drew out the first. "Here is my portion."

Noah said, "You have drawn the middle of the earth. You are indeed blessed because three holy places fall in your land: the Holy of Holies in the Temple, Mount Sinai, and Mount Zion. Your land will be neither hot nor cold."

Then Noah turned to Ham. "You may draw next. Then Japheth."

Ham drew the stone that designated his portion as the south, which was hot. Then Japheth drew the stone for the north, which was cold. Then Noah said to them, "Now we have divided one hundred and four lands and ninety-nine islands. Japheth has forty-four lands, thirty-three islands, twenty-two languages, and five kinds of writing. Ham has thirty-four lands, thirty-three islands, twenty-four languages, and five kinds of writing. And Shem has twenty-six lands, thirty-three islands, twenty-six languages, and six kinds of writing."

"Shem has one more kind of writing than Japheth and I," said Ham.

"The extra set is Hebrew. Because Shem has the three holy places where the Hebrew language is used, so he must have the Hebrew writing. Now go, my sons, cultivate your lands and rebuild the world."

So Ham went to the south, Japheth to the north, and Shem stayed in the central part of the world. Each one worked hard building new houses and roads and walls of cities, constructing new bridges over rivers, cultivating the land for food. They grew trees for their fruit and shade, and they raised flowers for their beauty.

One day, while Shem was working in his garden, Noah came to him and said, "My son, there are certain plants in your garden which are good for food and others which are medicine for illnesses. Now I wish to show you which are the healing plants. See, here is the plant that will cure measles. And here is the herb that will heal scarlet fever. And here is the one that will ease the mumps. Study these plants. From your study will come the science of medicine. This new science must be used for the good of all people everywhere.

"Now, write down everything I teach you about these healing plants. You will then have the world's first medical book."

Shem gathered the leaves of the papyrus plant, which grew by the river bank, and pressed them together into sheets of paper. For a pen he used the spine of a stiff feather, plucked from a goose's tail. For ink he took the black galls that grew on the bark of an oak tree and soaked them in water. Then he wrote down everything that Noah taught him: the names of the healing plants, how to treat scratches, how to bandage a wound, and how to cure a cough.

"Now Shem," said Noah, "from this book people will learn how to cure their illnesses. Take it and learn everything that is in it; then give the book to your son to study. Then he will teach it to his son. Thus, from generation to generation, will people learn how to cure their sicknesses."

For many years Noah and his sons went on with their task of rebuilding the world. Though the work was hard, they were glad to do it. Then one day, when Noah returned from visiting his sons, he said to his wife, "Our sons have worked hard and have accomplished a great deal. I know that their work will last because God promised that never again would a flood cover the whole earth. I have faith in God's word. But human beings are weak creatures. We need a sign, something that we can point to and say, 'This is what God has given us as a reminder of the promise never again to cover all the earth with flood waters.' Of course, faith should be great enough to need no signs, but, until people learn that God brings only good to the earth, even in punishment, perhaps they do need some reassurance. I wonder if God will ever give us such a sign."

As Noah finished speaking, the sun went behind a cloud. A light rain began to fall. Then, while the rain still fell, the cloud moved away from the sun's face so that it shone through the raindrops.

"Look at the bow in the sky!" exclaimed Noah. "This rainbow must be God's sign that never again will the waters destroy the earth!"

Thus was the rainbow created, a thing of beauty which gives the promise to all humanity that, in the midst of trouble, life can still be safe and strong and that God is merciful. While the rain of sorrow falls in every life, in every life too the sun will cause a rainbow to shine and bring peace and hope.

Commentary

I have set My bow in the clouds, and it shall serve as a sign of the covenant between Me and the earth.   Genesis 9:13

*   *   *

Many of the stories in the Bible, especially in Genesis, and in the legends of the rabbis are concerned with origins: the creation of the world, the first man, the first woman, demons, fire. The story of Noah concludes with the first covenant between God and all living creatures. God promises not to destroy the world again by flood, and the rainbow is created to establish this covenant. (Gen. 9:16–17)

*   *   *

The story of Noah also provides the origin of the nations of the world. According to rabbinic legend, the three sons of Noah each went off to initiate a different nation, much as the twelve sons of Jacob represent the twelve tribes of Israel. Ham founded the nations of Africa; Japheth the nations of the north; and Shem the nations of the Middle East, including Israel.

*   *   *

The Midrash attributes to Noah the ability to tell which plants and herbs could serve as food and which as medicine. Throughout the Midrash the rabbis give the origins not only of life's necessities but also of such ornamental practices as wearing makeup and jewelry, which were said to have been taught to women by the "sons of God" in Genesis 6. Legend holds that the "sons of God" were two angels, Shemhazai and Azazel, who descended to earth, took human women for wives, and revealed many of the secrets of heaven. (*Yalkut Shimoni*, Gen. 44) This legend also establishes the origin of the evil generation that God decided to destroy at the time of Noah.

Write Your Own Midrash

The stories in Genesis and in the Midrash provide the explanations for the origins of many things: the origin of heaven and earth, of day and night, of fire, of all the languages and nations of the world. Make up a midrash about the origin of something. Describe how it came into being, what the circumstances were, or to whom it happened. Perhaps you can even combine several origin stories into one.

✤ 5 ✤

The Wonderful Child

After the ark came to rest, the sons of Noah and their families each went off to different parts of the world and fathered nations. In the generations after the Flood, when people again multiplied throughout the earth, they were ruled by Nimrod, a mighty hunter who became king. At that time everyone spoke the same language. Together they decided to build a great tower to heaven *"to make a name for ourselves."* (Gen. 11:4) God punished them for this Tower of Babel by confusing their languages and by scattering them over the face of the earth. According to the Midrash, one of those who lived during the building of the Tower of Babel refused to have anything to do with it, considering it a form of idolatry. This was Abraham. The history of the Jewish people begins with his story since he was the first Jew.

Nimrod, a harsh and cruel king, ruled his country without mercy. He scorned the True God, worshiped idols, and forced all his subjects to do likewise. He would often order his idol-makers to make new images and force his people to worship them.

But one day he changed his mind about making new gods. Since his subjects would give their loyalty to any god that he

chose and since he was the most powerful man on earth, why shouldn't he, Nimrod the king, also be a god? The more he thought of that idea, the better he liked it; in fact, he considered it a stroke of genius. So he issued a decree:

"Henceforth, Nimrod the Mighty is the god of the whole world!
Hereafter, all people must bow down to him, and him alone must they worship!"

The people read the proclamation and obediently followed its commands. Nimrod enjoyed his new role, and, as each day passed, the people worshiped him more and more. Soon he came to believe that he had not made himself a god but that he actually had been born a god!

Day by day he set himself farther and farther away from common things, as befits a god. Thus he grew more blinded to what was truth and what was fantasy.

One night, as he lay sleeping, Nimrod had a dream that shook him with anger. Even in his sleep he realized his anger and forced himself awake to shout his rage aloud. Though it was the middle of the night, he summoned his counselors. They came, half-asleep but shivering with excitement to be awakened and commanded to the great presence of the god-king in the dark hours of the night. They didn't dare ask each other what might be wrong but waited for Nimrod to speak. When he did, his voice was harsh and haughty.

"I am your king and god. Listen to me. Last night I dreamed of a male child soon to be born who would one day prove that I am not god."

"Oh, a terrifying dream," murmured one counselor.

"Oh, an evil dream," whispered another.

"This dream shall never come true!" Nimrod shouted. "I shall prevent it! From this moment on, all male babies that are born shall be slain at birth."

A subdued murmur arose among the counselors.

"Quiet!" commanded Nimrod. "Does anyone dare question my wishes?"

"Oh, no," spoke up one of the bolder of the counselors. "But, Your Highness, what about baby girls?"

"My dream spoke of a male child. Female children may live," said Nimrod, "but all boy babies must be slain."

So the counselors went all over the kingdom proclaiming the heartless order of the king. The people would have rebelled at destroying their children at birth, but the many long years of worshiping false idols had dulled their wits. Because they never bothered to think out any problems for themselves, they questioned nothing, not even something so dreadful as this new and cruel decree. They worshiped Nimrod as king and god. If he told them to destroy their children, destroy them they would.

Now in that country there lived a man by the name of Terah, who was one of Nimrod's staunchest followers. Shortly after the decree of death to boy babies had been issued, Terah's wife, Emetel, gave birth to a little boy. Fortunately her husband wasn't home when the baby, Abraham, was born. To save her baby, Emetel decided to hide him.

"Oh, my poor little baby," she said to herself. "I must hide him so no one, not even his father, will know he has been born. His father worships Nimrod so much that he would betray even his innocent little son to the wicked king, and Nimrod would surely slay my child. I shall hide him where no one can find him."

She searched every room of the house for a safe hiding-place, but she found none.

"If I cannot hide him in my house," she decided, "then I shall have to find a place somewhere else."

So, early the next morning, before it was light, she crept quietly out of her house, covering little Abraham in blankets. On her feet she wore sandals of velvet so that no one would hear her walking. She walked along the road for several hours until she found a cave.

"This is a good hiding-place. No one knows about this cave but me. But I must leave him here alone because, if I stay with him, someone will notice my absence. They will look for me and find my baby and put him to death. So I shall have to go home and pretend that I have no child at all."

She laid him down gently on some grass that she gathered and formed into a little bed. Then she kissed her sleeping baby and quietly stole away.

Now this baby was not an ordinary child. He was the one whom God had sent down to earth to teach people the true religion of the world. Therefore God performed many miracles for the infant Abraham.

After his mother left, the child slept for a while. When he awoke, it was dark in the cave. He was hungry and began to cry. Seeing that the baby had no one to take care of him, God said to the angel Gabriel, "Gabriel, go down to that cave where the newborn Abraham lies alone and uncared for, and take care of him."

Gabriel flew down to the cave. The baby was still crying. Although Gabriel picked him up, the baby still cried. Gabriel realized he must be hungry. He let the baby suck his finger, from which flowed a fountain of sweet milk. When the infant drank all he wanted, the fountain stopped flowing.

The next miracle occurred when Abraham was ten days old. By that time, instead of being a helpless infant, he was already able to walk, talk, and take care of himself. At the end of those ten days he looked and acted like a young man. Since Abraham could now take care of himself completely, Gabriel left him and returned to heaven.

When Abraham was alone once more, he walked about the edge of the valley, observing the world. All of it was very new and interesting and he gazed for hours in wonder. At night he saw millions of stars in the sky, some twinkling, some shining with a clear, white light. He clapped his hands and exclaimed, "Why, these stars must be the gods!" After staring at the stars for a while, he said, "Yes, these stars must surely be the gods. I shall worship them."

As he was about to bow down and pay homage to them, the night ended, the stars began to fade, the dawn came, and the stars disappeared. Then Abraham said, "Those stars cannot be the gods if they can fade away like that. No, I will not worship them."

Then the sun came out, shining strongly and brightly, casting a golden glow on the world, and giving forth heat and light. Abraham, shielding his eyes from its glare, lifted up his face to feel the warmth of the sun. He said, "This surely must be the god I will worship."

Then, after several hours, the day came to an end; the sun set in the west and sank beyond the horizon out of sight. Its bright golden blaze vanished, leaving the world dull and dismal. And Abraham said, "How can the sun be god? Like the stars, it too disappears, leaving the world gloomy and dark."

While Abraham was talking, the moon rose in the east and, attracted by the pale gleam of its light, he turned to look at it.

"How gently the moon sheds its light over the earth. It brings a feeling of calmness, the promise of peace. It must be god. I will worship it."

But as he spoke a cloud covered the face of the moon, and Abraham, again in the darkness of night, said, "If so small a thing as a cloud can cover up the moon's light, if a wisp of vapor can extinguish its beauty, then the moon cannot be god. Not the stars nor the sun nor the moon—none of these is god. I was ready to worship each of them. But I know there must be One greater than they who has created all of them, the stars and the sun and the moon and everything on earth.

"There is only one God and that one God alone will I worship."

Commentary

I will make of you a great nation, and I will bless you.

Genesis 12:2

*   *   *

More than any other patriarch or sage, Abraham aroused the curiosity of the rabbis, who wanted to discover as much as they could about his childhood. It was Abraham, after all, who realized that there was only one God. Because the Torah says nothing about Abraham's childhood, the rabbis read between the lines and imagined a childhood for him, modeled exactly on that of Moses. That is how the Midrash works—the solution to any mystery can always be found in the Torah since it contains all truths. Thus Nimrod (rather than Pharaoh), fearing a prophecy foretold in the stars, orders all firstborn boys to be slain. Abraham's mother leaves her child in a cave as Moses' mother left him in a basket floating on the Nile.

The baby boy is kept alive in the cave by the angel Gabriel, who uses his thumb to feed him milk. The boy grows to Bar Mitzvah age in less than two weeks, educated by the angel in the ways of the Torah and with a strong love of God. The mother returns and finds the cave empty. Seeing the boy standing nearby, she asks him if he has seen an infant. For a moment, the boy rebukes her for abandoning her child, but, soon afterward, reveals that he is Abraham and tells her of his miraculous growth, aided by the angel. (*Sefer Hayashar* and *Pirke de-Rabbi Eliezer*) Since Abraham and Moses are the most important patriarchs, the rabbis linked them through stories. Ironically, Moses, who lived in a later period, serves as the model for Abraham.

That is possible because past and present merge in rabbinic legend into one timeless and all encompassing present.

Write Your Own Midrash

One of the great mysteries about Abraham is how he discovered that there is only one God in all the world. The rabbis offer several legends about how this happened, but there could be other explanations. Perhaps you have considered this question and have your own answer. If so, write a midrash in which you attribute your own insights to Abraham. Abraham was the first Jew, but he lived in a time before the Torah was given. What would Abraham have thought if he had been able to read the Torah? What would he have had to say to Moses, who carried the torch in his generation just as Abraham had in his. Imagine a meeting between Abraham and Moses and what they would say. Since past and present exist at the same time in the Midrash, and those in one generation often meet those in another, this is perfectly proper.

⚡6⚡

The Garden in the Fire

Nothing is told in Genesis about the childhood of Abraham. This frustrated the rabbis, for Abraham's importance in Jewish history is preeminent. They longed to know how he came to the understanding that there is only one God. So too, they wished for Abraham to have a heroic childhood as so many heroes in myth and legend have. These longings gave birth to many legends about the young Abraham, which fill the gaps in the biblical narrative.

Abraham walked along the road thinking deep thoughts. How strange is the world which the Great Power had created; how hard it is for us to understand its wonders and its mysteries. How was it that the sun and moon never bumped into each other? How was it that ground was made firm to walk on and water buoyant to float on? How was it that trees reached towards the sky and snails crawled among rocks? And how was it that human beings were formed so perfectly, with muscles that held bones together, and a skin to cover them all, and especially with minds that can think these thoughts and be grateful to God who had wrought such perfection?

With these musings filling him with awe and wonderment,

he walked along until he came to his parents' home. He stood at the door and heard the sound of weeping and talking from within. He listened and overheard a conversation.

"O Terah, my husband," he heard a woman say, "I have a confession to make. A baby boy was born to us ten days ago. Fearing that Nimrod's soldiers would put him to death, I took our child and hid him."

"Where did you hide him?" Abraham heard the man ask.

"In a cave. All alone in a cave. And now I'm afraid the poor baby must have perished with no one to take care of him and feed him." She wept bitterly.

Then Abraham understood that this was the home of his father and his mother. He knocked on the door and said, "Let me enter. This is your son Abraham."

Terah and his wife were so astonished when they opened the door and saw him standing there that they could hardly talk.

"You, my son Abraham!" his mother said. "Why, my son was an infant. He would be ten days old. You are a young man."

"But I am he. I am Abraham."

"Is this magic?" asked Terah. "How can you be so grown up in ten days?"

"It is one of God's miracles," answered Abraham. "He took care of me and made me grow quickly."

"What god do you mean?" asked Terah.

"The God in heaven," answered Abraham, "the only God of the world."

"The god in heaven," Terah said. "Why bother with one so far away? I have idols right here in my own home. I made them myself. It's easier to worship gods you can see. Besides, I worship our king, Nimrod, who is the god of the whole earth."

"Oh, the king!" cried Abraham's mother. "Oh, I had forgotten all about him. Now he will know about our child and will put him to death!"

"Don't worry," Terah said. "Can't you see that Abraham is

safe from Nimrod now? He is a young man. Nimrod will never guess that he is only ten days old. He is in no danger."

His mother wept for joy, his father beamed with pleasure, and Abraham was glad, except that something his father said had disturbed him. Abraham asked Terah, "Did you say, my father, that Nimrod is a god? He is only a man like yourself. How can you worship him? Also, how can you worship idols that are made of wood and stone? Can't you see that the idol you make has a mouth but cannot speak? It has eyes but cannot see. It has ears but cannot hear. It has feet but cannot walk. It is nothing but stone or wood. I worship the True God, the God of us all."

"I don't know anything about your true god," Terah said.

"How can you not know about God?" Abraham asked. "All the world tells of the one Creator who made the world. All of it speaks of God's plan. All nature lives in harmony. The winter doesn't come with the heat of the sun. The summer doesn't come with icy blasts of wind. The buds of the trees flower and dry up and are born again. All of them declare the wisdom of the God who made them. It's true we cannot see God, we see only God's work, but God sees everything and knows what is in every heart."

"Oh, you are a child," Terah said. "What do you know about such things? Don't worry me with your chatter."

The next day, Terah told Abraham to bring him some pieces of oak wood to make an idol. Abraham went into the forest, gathered the wood, and brought it to his father. He watched closely while Terah carved out of the wood a little doll which he called a god. When it was finished, he named it Barisat.

"Father," said Abraham, "why should you worship this little wooden doll which you just made with your own hands? It seems to me that this idol should worship *you* because you created *it*."

"How dare you call my god a little doll?" Terah said. "You are disrespectful. Be still." Abraham grew silent but kept watching his father. "Now," said Terah, "I shall place Barisat next to the fire where my food is cooking. Barisat," he said to the wooden image, "watch the fire for me. See that it doesn't go out. Watch the food until it is cooked."

Then Terah left the house, but Abraham was curious about the little idol. So, he stood there, watching it. It had been placed too close to the fire, and the flames began to lick at it. Before Abraham could pull it out, it was half-burned. He made no attempt to rescue it but watched it being completely destroyed.

By then the food was cooked, and Terah was in the dining room ready for his dinner. Abraham carried it into him. When he set it down in front of him, Terah blessed another one of his gods, Marumath.

"You shouldn't bless your god Marumath, Father," Abraham said. "It was Barisat who fell into the fire, thus adding more fuel with which to cook your food."

"Oh, did Barisat get burned up? That's too bad, but I'll make another god like him later. Now don't bother me. Let me enjoy my meal."

Abraham began to laugh. "Oh, Father, why bless either one of these idols? Fire is more to be worshiped than idols made of wood and stone because the fire can destroy them."

"Then perhaps I shall worship the fire," said Terah.

"You cannot worship fire either because water can quench the fire."

"Then I shall worship the water," said Terah.

"How can you worship water when the earth can soak it up?"

"Then I shall worship the earth."

"The sun can dry up the earth," said Abraham. "So you should not worship the earth."

"Then I shall worship the sun."

"The sun is not to be worshiped either. The light of the sun goes out when the darkness comes."

"Oh, you are a stubborn boy, Abraham," cried his father in

vexation. "You say I cannot worship idols made of wood or stone. You say I cannot worship fire or water or earth or sun. What then can I worship?"

"The True God," answered Abraham, "who made the heaven and the earth and human beings."

"No, no, don't fool me with stories of your god whom I cannot even see," Terah said. "Your god, you say, lives in heaven where no one can ever see him. Now, you come with me. I shall show you the *real* gods."

So he took Abraham into his temple where there were twelve great idols and a number of little ones, perhaps fifty altogether. "Here are the idols," Terah said, "who have made everything you see on earth. They even created me and all other human beings."

He bowed down before his gods. He praised them. He called them holy and powerful. Then he rose from his knees, told the names of each god to Abraham, and said, "You stay here, my son. Study these gods and see for yourself how great they are. Then you will forget your strange god who keeps himself too far away in the heavens to be seen by anyone."

Terah left the temple. Abraham, left alone with the false gods, said to himself, "Now I am going to be fair. I will give my father's gods every chance to prove whether they have any value except the wood and stones from which they were made."

So he walked up to the statue whose name was Zucheus. He bowed low before it and said, "O Zucheus, if you are truly a god, then speak to me. Say something, and I promise to be your servant for all time."

He stood silent and waited. Zucheus remained dumb. He did not say one word.

"Perhaps I have not praised you enough, O Zucheus," Abraham said. "Listen to me, god of my father. I bow down before you. I praise you as the creator of the world. To you will I give my homage. You are all-powerful, all-merciful, all-wonderful. Now, O Zucheus, speak to your servant Abraham."

But Zucheus, who was made of stone, kept a stony silence.

Abraham laughed. "Oh, indeed, you are no god or you would speak one word to make me your slave." He laughed again. "Of stone my father made you. Of stone you remain, but a god you are not."

Then Abraham walked to another idol whose name was Joauv. It was made of silver and beautifully ornamented. There were rubies and emeralds in his crown. His eyes were onyx and his hands ivory. Abraham bowed low to Joauv and said, "O Joauv, you are one of my father's gods. Give me a sign that you are really a god and not just a statue of silver and precious stone, and I, Abraham, will become your loyal slave forever. Walk, Joauv. Move your silvery legs and walk."

But Joauv glinted in the sunlight and did not take a step.

"Hah, you are no god. You are only a piece of silver which my father fashioned into a statue."

Abraham walked from one idol to another. This one he asked to speak, that one to see, this one to walk, but they all remained motionless, blind, and silent like the lifeless statues they were.

Then Abraham stood at the front of the temple and spoke to all the statues together, "Oh, you idols of wood and stone, of silver and gold and precious jewels, you are only playthings which my father and his neighbors make with their own hands. And you they worship as gods.

"Now listen to me, Abraham, the child of the Living God. I have asked you to perform no miracles. I have asked you only to show me that you live, that you breathe, that you speak, that you are anything more than wood and stone and silver. But wooden you are, stonily silent you are, and silent you will remain."

He walked around, poking each idol with his finger as he talked. "But I am greater than you all. Even when I was an abandoned baby, alone in the cave, I cried a little, and God in heaven heard me, sending the angel Gabriel to feed me and to watch over me. I am alive and I worship the Living God. You are only the idle boasts of stupid people."

Then Abraham picked up a hatchet and went about the temple

breaking up all the idols. He smashed Nahor with one blow; he broke Marumath with two chops; with three sweeps he destroyed Zucheus. And then, when he had broken every statue, he put the hatchet into the hand of the biggest idol, the one called Joauv.

Almost immediately, Terah, his father, came running in. "What is wrong? I heard stone smashing. I heard the chopping of wood. What has happened?"

"Look, Father," said Abraham. "Joauv, your god of silver, has broken up all your idols."

"You are lying, you wicked child! This is your mischief!" Terah shouted. "Why have you broken my idols?"

"Truly I did not do it," Abraham said teasingly. "Joauv did it. I'll tell you why. I asked your idols to speak to me, to walk, to move. They could not since they are made of wood and stone. I suppose Joauv must have been angry because they would not show their power, and he took this hatchet and broke them all up."

Terah shouted at his son, "You know that you lie, Abraham. These gods are only wood and stone. I made them myself. There is no soul or power in them to do what you say they have done. I know that they cannot move or speak or use a hatchet. It was you who used it. You broke up my idols, and you have put the hatchet into the hand of Joauv."

Without a further word, Terah turned around and stalked out of the temple. As he walked towards the palace, his angry thoughts kept tumbling over in his mind: Nimrod was his king, his god, and to him Terah owed his first loyalty; Abraham was his son, but, by destroying the idols, he had proved himself an unfaithful son and a disobedient subject to Nimrod. "Yes," said Terah to himself, "Abraham must be punished and to Nimrod I must go and tell the story."

When the king heard the story, he could not control his anger, and he shouted, "Bring this wicked Abraham here before me!"

Four guards went to Terah's house, seized Abraham, and brought him to the palace.

"What have you done to your father's gods?" Nimrod demanded.

"Nothing," said Abraham. And he told Nimrod the very same story he had told his father: The big god Joauv had broken all the little gods because Joauv was ashamed that they would not or could not walk or think or talk.

"Don't tell me lies," shouted Nimrod. "You know as well as I do that idols do not speak nor do they eat nor do they move. How then could Joauv have destroyed the other idols?"

"Then, O King, if your gods do nothing," Abraham answered, "how can you worship them? You should worship God, who alone is the King of the universe and has power over every creature in the world."

"I am the king of the universe!" shouted Nimrod, his face getting purple with rage. "I alone have power over every creature in the world! Guards!" he shrieked. And two fierce guards stepped forward. "Guards! Seize this wretch! Bind him and throw him into the pit. Give him nothing to eat. Let him starve to death."

The guards seized Abraham roughly, bound him tightly with ropes, and threw him into a deep pit—black, cold, and damp. But Abraham did not struggle or plead for he was not afraid. He knew that somehow God would take care of him. So he prayed, "O God of the universe, see the suffering of Your son Abraham and rescue him from the wicked Nimrod."

As once before, when Abraham needed miraculous help, it was Gabriel who came. He flew down into the pit and lived with Abraham for one whole year. During that time he supplied him with fresh water and all kinds of food, and Abraham remained strong and healthy.

After Abraham had been in the pit for a year, Satan, who loved only evil and evildoers, discovered that Abraham was still alive. Fearing Abraham's possible influence on the people of the earth and knowing that Abraham could not be persuaded to become an idolator like everyone else, Satan decided Abraham must die.

Disguised as one of Nimrod's counselors, Satan went to him and said, "O Nimrod, I wonder if the evil Abraham, who will not worship you and whom you threw into the pit months ago, still lives. If he does, someday he will bring you and your kingdom to ruin. If he is still alive, you should bring him out of the pit and burn him to death."

"Oh, he must be dead by now," Nimrod laughed. "But we shall see. If, by any chance, he is still alive, we'll burn him as you suggest."

One of Nimrod's counselors laughed. "Oh, Abraham cannot possibly be alive. He must surely be dead. He has been in the pit for one whole year without any food or water."

"Well, we shall see," Nimrod said. "Guard!" he shouted. Two huge guards stepped forward. "Go to the pit where you threw the wicked Abraham and bring him out. If he is dead, we shall throw him to the vultures. If he is alive, we shall throw him into a huge fire and burn him up."

The king, his counselors, Satan, the court followers—everybody followed the two guards until they came to the pit. They looked in and saw only Abraham because Gabriel had already departed. The taller guard, who was as tall as a giant, reached down into the pit, grabbed hold of Abraham's shoulder, and pulled him out. Everyone cried aloud in surprise when they saw him.

"Look how strong he is!" cried one counselor.

"He is the healthiest looking person I've ever seen," cried another.

"I was afraid he was alive!" muttered Satan.

King Nimrod cried the loudest of all. "What! Are you still alive? Who gave you the food that kept you living? Come, tell me, who gave you the food?"

"The unseen God of the world sent me food," Abraham answered.

"Bah!" Nimrod sneered. "There is no unseen god. *I* am god."

"You are no god," said Abraham.

"Quiet!" shrieked Nimrod. "Quiet, you wicked man, you breaker of idols, you destroyer of the gods. Guards! Build a big fire, a huge fire, the biggest fire the world has ever seen!"

The guards hastened to do his bidding. It took two days to build this fire. Twenty men chopped wood for one whole day, and, when they were through piling it up, it reached almost to the tops of the trees.

"Now light the fire," Nimrod ordered.

One of the guards took a flaming torch and touched it to the wood. First a little flame flickered. Then all the wood caught fire at once, and a powerful flame shot up towards the clouds.

Abraham's mother was there in the crowd, and she cried to him, "Oh, my son, bow quickly before Nimrod and tell him you are sorry and he will release you, or you will surely be destroyed by this terrible fire."

But Abraham said, "Do not worry, dear mother. I trust in God."

Then his mother said, "Then may the God whom you worship rescue you from Nimrod's fire."

"Don't delay!" shouted Nimrod. "Throw him into the fire."

The two guards came forward to grasp Abraham's arms. As they lifted him off his feet, Abraham looked up at the sky and cried, "O God, save me from this evil king and this flaming fire."

Up in heaven, Gabriel said to God, "What will You do now about Abraham? Can You let him die?"

God said, "Never fear. I shall rescue him."

Then God spoke to the fire, "O Fire, cool off and do not burn My servant Abraham."

At that instant the two guards threw Abraham into the fire. As he was falling into the flames, all the wood in the fire stopped burning. Instead, some of the logs burst into buds. Some of the wood became cherry trees, some apple trees, some peach trees. Some of it turned into roses, some into violets, some into peonies.

In a twinkling the huge pile of firewood that reached almost to the tops of the trees became a wondrous garden of living trees and fragrant flowers, with birds flying about, caroling their sweet songs. In the middle of the garden sat Abraham, eating a peach from the peach tree and holding a red rose. And around him sat a company of the heavenly hosts, singing hymns of praise to God.

When Nimrod saw the fire change into the beautiful garden, he grew purple with anger and shouted, "This is magic! This is witchcraft!"

Now some of his followers found the courage to answer him.

"No, Nimrod," they said. "This is not witchcraft. This is not magic. We see now that this is the wondrous power of the Living God, beside whom there is no other god, and that Abraham is God's mighty servant."

Nimrod's counselors, the court followers, the princes, and all the people fell on their knees before Abraham and began to worship him. Nimrod was helpless. He shouted at the people to stop worshiping Abraham, but that did not stop them. Abraham stopped them.

"Do not bend your knee before me," he said, "or any other human being. Bow down only before God, the Ruler of the universe who created you. Follow God's commands, be merciful, and do good. It was God who delivered me from the fire."

Thus it was around the edge of the miraculous garden that Abraham taught the people to worship God.

Commentary

And he built an altar there to the Lord.　　　　Genesis 13:18

* * *

This legend is so famous that most people think it appears in the Bible—until they try to find it. The story of Abraham and the idols supplies a central incident in Abraham's childhood after he realizes that there is only one God and that his father's idols are useless. (*Sefer Hayashar*) Demonstrating the foolishness of idolatry is a common theme in rabbinic sources. This story combines two famous legends about the child Abraham. The second tale shows Abraham fulfilling the prophecy that one day he would overthrow King Nimrod. Here Nimrod has young Abraham cast into a pit, where for one year he is sustained by an angel. When Abraham is found alive, Nimrod has him thrown into a giant furnace. Instead of burning, however, the wood of the furnace blossoms, turning into a garden. (*Sefer Hayashar*)

The episode of the pit is clearly drawn from the incident of Joseph being thrown into the pit by his brothers. (In another legend Jethro is said to have thrown Moses into a pit, where for ten years he was sustained by Zippora, who secretly gave him food and drink.) This experience in a pit becomes a symbol for the suffering and difficulties these patriarchs undergo. They survive by holding true to their faith.

Write Your Own Midrash

In the Midrash the boy Abraham is portrayed as a great hero whose powerful faith in God enables him to conquer any foe. Write some additional adventures in which young Abraham overcomes other enemies. Feel free to include miracles since these are so often found in the Midrash, as in the case of the furnace that blossoms into a garden. Since Abraham was said to live in the time of the Tower of Babel, he might have a confrontation with the tower's builders, who, according to the Midrash, were great idolators. He might also have other confrontations with his archenemy, King Nimrod.

✢ 7 ✢

The Sheltering Cloud

In their old age, Abraham and his wife Sarah were blessed with a child, Isaac. One day God tested Abraham by commanding him to take Isaac to Mount Moriah and sacrifice him upon an altar. Although all of Abraham's hopes for the future depended on Isaac, Abraham did as he was told. When he was about to sacrifice his son, an angel stopped him. God had recognized Abraham's complete devotion. A ram was sacrificed instead, and, in Jewish history, this event signifies the end of human sacrifice. When Sarah died, shortly after the return from Mount Moriah, Abraham purchased the cave of Machpelah as her gravesite. Abraham, who by that time was an old man, then decided to find a wife for Isaac.

Sarah, the mother of Isaac, was beloved by God and respected by all people. Even her name set her apart as one who is unusual. Sarah means "princess." During her lifetime, three signs distinguished Sarah as a noble woman.

The gates of her tent always stood wide open. It was an invitation to hungry people to come and share her food. No one left her door empty-handed.

Inside her tent, a light burned steadily. It never went out.

Nor could human breath blow it out. It was not made of tallow like a candle, nor of any earthly matter. It was a heavenly light sent to show that in Sarah's heart and mind the love of learning flamed.

And above her tent hovered the Sheltering Cloud. This was God's special sign to show Sarah's gentle protectiveness over all people who needed help. All who saw it knew that God watched over the first matriarch of Israel, Mother Sarah.

When she became very old, Sarah died. At the moment her soul broke free from her body, the eternal light in her tent went out, the doors shut fast and would not open, the Sheltering Cloud broke up and vanished into the sky. All the blessings that were hers in life departed with her.

When Abraham and Isaac mourned for her, all the people grieved with them.

After some years had passed, Abraham said to Isaac, "You and I, my son, still mourn the absence of your mother. Never will we be happy until you find a wife as noble as your mother to bring God's blessings back to her tent."

Then Abraham summoned his faithful servant, Eliezer, and said, "The time has come for my son to get married. I have three companions, Aner, Eshcol, and Mamre. Each one has a daughter. I must choose the daughter of one of these friends to be Isaac's wife."

Before Eliezer could answer, God spoke, "Listen to Me, Abraham! Listen to My words. Your son Isaac will marry, but his wife will not be the daughter of Aner or Eshcol or Mamre. I have already chosen Isaac's wife. In the land of Haran lives your brother Nahor. His wife is Milcah. Milcah and Nahor have a son, Bethuel. And Bethuel has a daughter whose name is Rebecca. She is the wife I have chosen for Isaac."

Abraham turned to Eliezer in excitement. "You have heard, Eliezer! My niece Rebecca has been chosen to be Isaac's wife! Now, to you, my trusted friend, will I give this task: Go to Haran and bring back Rebecca to marry my son. Upon your return I shall reward you well."

"I seek no gifts from you," said Eliezer. "I am glad to do anything you ask."

"Nevertheless, you shall have your reward. When you return from Haran with Rebecca, I shall set you free. No more will you be a slave."

"O my master, you are most gracious!" exclaimed Eliezer. "You have always been kind to me. It has been a joy to serve you. Yet, I shall be happy to be a free man."

"You shall surely be free. Now go and do my bidding."

Abraham and Eliezer chose ten of Abraham's finest camels and loaded them with ten boxes of jewels. There were diamond and ruby rings, jade and emerald bracelets, brocades and tapestries, and fine woolens. All these jewels and fine cloths were to be gifts to Rebecca and her family.

When the ten boxes were loaded on the ten camels, Abraham selected his ten most trusted guards to go with Eliezer on his dangerous trip across the desert. As the caravan was about to start out, two angels appeared.

"Eliezer," said the angels, "God has sent us to guard you on your way across the desert. On your way back we will watch over you and Rebecca."

"Then we shall surely be safe," said Eliezer.

So, with the ten boxes on the ten camels, guarded by the ten watchmen, accompanied by the two heavenly messengers, Eliezer set out across the desert. This journey should have lasted for seventeen days, but, so the story goes, a miracle occurred. As the caravan trudged across the shifting sands, it seemed to Eliezer that the earth rushed forward to meet him. The miles rolled under his feet, and only a few hours passed before he reached Haran. Instead of arriving tired and worn out from a long trek of many days, he was fresh and strong.

But he was thirsty. The sweltering sun blazed hot over the desert and even in those few hours his throat grew parched and dry. So he went directly to the well.

Every town had one well from which the people drew their supply of water. To this well every evening came all the young girls. They came singing their songs, a picturesque sight in their long sweeping skirts of different colors. Each girl carried her water pitcher on her left shoulder and balanced it with her right hand.

Eliezer watched the chattering girls draw water from the well and said to the two angels, "Rebecca is the girl I must find. I shall pray that God will give me a sign by which I shall recognize her. There is the well, and there are the young girls drawing water. I am thirsty. I shall ask them for water. Let the sign be that Rebecca shall be the only one to give me water to drink. That is how I shall know her."

He walked closer to the well. He said to one girl, "Please give me water for I am thirsty."

But she said, "No. I must take this water home."

Then he said to another girl, "Please give me water. My thirst is great."

But she said, "No. I must take this water home."

Then he said to still another girl, "Please give me water. My thirst is very great."

But she said, "No. I must take this water home."

One by one the girls refused to give him water. When the last girl had turned away, up to the well stepped the loveliest young girl Eliezer had ever seen. She wore a long white dress that swayed as she walked. Her long black hair was silky and thick. Her eyes were big and black, and she had a sweet and beautiful face.

Eliezer said to her, "Please give me water for I am thirsty."

"Surely," she said, smiling at him. "I shall give you and your camels water to drink." She drew water from the well and filled her pitcher. Then she handed it to Eliezer. "Here is the pitcher. Drink all you need. I shall fill the trough for the camels."

"I thank you," Eliezer said, taking the pitcher and drinking from it. "You are very kind. What is your name?"

"My name is Rebecca. My father is called Bethuel, the son of Milcah and Nahor."

Eliezer knew he had found the right girl. He said to her, "I am Eliezer. I have come from Canaan, from your uncle Abraham, to see your father."

"Oh! Is my uncle well? My father will be happy to see you. Come with me. I will take you to our home."

"You lead the way. I shall follow after you," said Eliezer. "But, before you go, I have a gift for you from your uncle." He pulled from his robe two bracelets. "These are for you."

"Oh, what beautiful bracelets!" said Rebecca, taking them. "It was kind of my uncle to send me a present. Thank you. Now I'll show you the way."

Because Eliezer had to lead his caravan, he sent the girl on ahead. She was fleet-footed and walked quickly, hurrying to tell her parents that Abraham's servant was coming. As she entered her home, she ran to her parents and her brother Laban. She told them about meeting Eliezer at the well, that he was coming to their home with ten camels and ten boxes and ten guards, and she showed them the bracelets he had given her.

Taking the bracelets in his hand, Laban, who loved only money, saw that they were precious. He wanted them for himself, but he knew he could not take them from Rebecca. He said to himself, "My sister said that this servant of my uncle has ten boxes; perhaps there are many precious objects in them; I shall go to meet this Eliezer and steal them from him."

So Laban sneaked out of the house and hurried down the road he knew Eliezer must take. He arrived at the stream and saw Eliezer on the other side with the ten camels and the ten servants. Because the camels were so heavily loaded, they could not go through the stream unguided. Eliezer, with his giant strength, picked up two camels at one time and carried them safely across. Then he went back for two more, then two more, and thus he continued until all the camels were on the other side.

Never had Laban seen such an exhibition of strength! He realized that this was a man of extraordinary physical powers, and he trembled. He knew he dared not engage in battle with him, or Eliezer might kill him with one blow. "I shall have to find other means of stealing the boxes," he said. And he pretended he came as a friend.

"Greetings, Eliezer!" cried Laban with false sweetness. "My sister Rebecca has told us of your arrival. I have come to welcome you and escort you to our home." He led them to the house, and at the door he said, "Enter with the blessings of God."

Now Abraham had told Eliezer that Laban was an idol worshiper who did not believe in God. On hearing him use God's name so insincerely, Eliezer wanted to rebuke him. However, he held his tongue because he wished to carry out his mission without trouble. He entered the house where he was welcomed by Bethuel, Rebecca's father, and her mother.

Then he ordered his ten servants to unload the camels and bring the ten boxes into Bethuel's house. Everyone cried out in surprise when they were opened. They were amazed at the sight of the brilliant jewels and costly woolens. But Eliezer did not, at once, tell them they were gifts.

Laban, unable to control his greed, pulled his father to one side and whispered, "Look at these treasures! Let's get them for ourselves! Let's poison this man!"

His father quickly agreed. Laban then stole into the dining room and poured some poison into the soup at the place where Eliezer was to sit. A few moments later, Rebecca's mother invited their guest to join them at dinner. As they were all sitting down, Eliezer bumped against the table and spilled the plate of poisoned soup.

"Oh, your soup is spilled," cried Laban, jumping up. "I'll bring you another."

"Don't bother," Eliezer said. "I'm really not hungry. Besides, I wish to tell you without delay what brings me here to Haran. Abraham, my master, desires Rebecca to return with me to Canaan to be the wife of his son Isaac."

"That is a great honor!" exclaimed Rebecca's mother.

"Not so fast," said her husband, Bethuel. "Perhaps Isaac is not worthy of my daughter."

Eliezer laughed. "You do not know Isaac, or you would not say that. My master's son is noble and God-fearing, a man of character. Here are documents which Abraham sent to show you that he has signed over all his possessions to Isaac. Someday Isaac will be a very rich man."

"But why does he come so far for a wife?" asked Laban. "Are there no young girls in Canaan?"

"Indeed there are many," said Eliezer. "Ishmael's and Lot's daughters and the daughters of Abraham's companions are all lovely girls. Isaac could marry any one of them, but his father wishes him to marry a daughter of this family."

"But Canaan is so far away," objected Bethuel. "Perhaps my daughter will not want to go away from her own country and her own people."

"Let Rebecca decide," said her mother.

Eliezer turned to the young girl who had listened silently to this conversation. "Will you come with me to the land of Canaan to become the wife of Isaac?"

Rebecca said, "Oh, yes. Happily shall I go with you."

Eliezer was delighted and Milcah her mother was glad and even her father and brother were content. Then Eliezer distributed to Rebecca and her family the gifts of diamonds and rubies and emeralds, brocades and tapestries, and fine woolens.

Rebecca and her mother went busily to the task of packing all the girl's clothes and belongings to take to her new home. When her boxes were packed, they were bound onto Eliezer's camels. Now Rebecca was ready to leave her home to go to Canaan and marry Isaac.

Eliezer watered the camels and saw that the ten guards were ready. Then he and Rebecca, accompanied by the camels, the servants, and the two angels, journeyed from Haran to Canaan.

This trip too was wonderfully shortened. With the help of the angels they moved so swiftly that the whole journey took only three hours.

As they were approaching Abraham's house, Isaac saw the clouds of dust the camels kicked up, and he knew that this must be Eliezer returning with his bride. Eager to see her, he hurried towards them. As he came close, Rebecca saw that he was a handsome man and that an angel of God was his companion. In her excitement she leaned too far to one side and fell off her camel.

She cried out in fear. Isaac heard her cry and saw her fall. He ran to her and picked her up from the ground. Luckily she was unhurt.

"Isaac, this is Rebecca," said Eliezer. "This is your bride."

They looked at each other, smiled, and fell in love at first sight. They completely forgot everyone around them. They just gazed at one another. Isaac knew at once that this young bride would bring honor to the tent of his mother, and proudly he led her there.

All the years since Sarah's death, the doors had remained closed, the eternal light was gone, and the Sheltering Cloud had not been seen. As Isaac led Rebecca towards the tent, she placed her fingers lightly on the doors. Instantly they flew open.

She smiled at Isaac, and he smiled at her. Then he led her through the doors, which were to remain open during her lifetime, to the tent of his mother. Rebecca stopped on the threshold. No lamps had been lighted inside. As she lifted her hand to draw the curtain aside and step within, slowly the darkness was pierced by a little light that grew larger and larger until the tent was filled with the eternal light that had burned so brightly in the days of Sarah.

As they stood gazing at the light, just before stepping inside, Rebecca lifted her head up to the sky and saw a wisp of cloud forming above them. The Sheltering Cloud settled over the tent which now was Rebecca's home!

"Oh, you are indeed worthy to take my mother's place," cried Isaac. "The open gate, the holy light shining within, and the Sheltering Cloud above are blessings that will shield you. Welcome to my mother's tent as my bride."

Thus did Rebecca follow in the footsteps of Sarah, the princess, the first mother of Israel.

Commentary

Go to the land of my birth and get a wife for my son Isaac.
                                                    Genesis 24:4

* * *

In the Midrash the death of Sarah is linked to the *Akedah,* the binding of Isaac on Mount Moriah. These two episodes follow each other in the text, and from the rabbinic perspective this is evidence that they are connected. The Midrash explains this link by describing how Satan showed Sarah a vision of what was taking place while Abraham and Isaac were on the mountain. So great was the shock that she died. Now Sarah was exceptionally pious, and, according to rabbinic tradition, the Divine Presence, the *Shechinah,* hovered at all times over her tent. This is the Sheltering Cloud of the story's title. The Divine Presence departs from Sarah's tent after her death and does not return until the arrival of Rebecca. Thus its appearance signifies that Rebecca is a worthy successor to Sarah and that God approves of the match between Rebecca and Isaac.

* * *

It is written in the Talmud that, forty days before a person is born, a voice goes forth out of heaven to announce that this one will be married to that one. (*Sotah* 2a) The Talmud adds that it is as difficult for God to complete these marriages as it was to split the waters of the Red Sea. This talmudic legend is echoed in this midrash about the betrothal of Isaac and Rebecca. The primary point of the midrash is to make their marriage seem fated. To this end it was necessary to eliminate the haphazard elements of the test that Eliezer gave to the girls coming to draw water at the well. Instead, God clearly announces that Rebecca is Isaac's destined one, and the rest of the legend simply becomes the fulfillment of this destiny.

* * *

The portrayal of Laban in the Midrash is even harsher than it is in the Bible. Of course the biblical Laban deceives Jacob into marrying Leah rather than Rachel and later chases after Jacob and Rachel when they leave together with their flocks and servants. But, while the biblical portrait of Laban is complex, acknowledging that he sheltered Jacob in a time of need, the midrashic view is one-sided. From the first kiss of Jacob and Laban, Laban was said to have searched Jacob's mouth for hidden pearls. This kind of treatment is typical of the figures the rabbis regarded as evil. Other figures whom the Midrash regards as villains include Ishmael, who is described by the rabbis as trying to shoot arrows at Isaac, and Esau, who is portrayed virtually as a beast.

* * *

Note that there is very little in the biblical text about Isaac. Except for the *Akedah* episode on Mount Moriah when he was a boy (although the Midrash describes Isaac as being forty years old at the time) and the moving description of the blessing he gives to Jacob (posing as Esau), the Bible tells little about his life. The Midrash, too, is surprisingly silent about the rest of Isaac's life. Perhaps the reason is that the rabbis needed to know the bare outlines of a life in order to fill in the missing narrative gaps, and in the case of Isaac this basic information is simply not known.

✳ ✳ ✳

One of the most obscure biblical figures is linked to the story of Rebecca and Isaac. The name Iscah, the sister of Milcah, Rebecca's mother, appears only once, in a genealogy. Because she belonged to a very important family, the rabbis were very curious about her. With nothing else to go on, they analyzed the root of her name, which means "to gaze" or "to prophesy." Based on this meaning, they determined that Iscah was a prophetess. And, in the Talmud, Iscah is identified with Sarah herself, "Rabbi Isaac observed: 'Iscah was Sarah, and why is she called Iscah? Because she foresaw the future by divine inspiration.'" (*Sanhedrin* 69b) This seems to suggest that, when Sarah would prophesy, she would become Iscah. This was the beginning of a long tradition of Sarah as a prophetess, with powers of divination even greater than those of Abraham.

Write Your Own Midrash

Sarah died before the marriage of her beloved son, Isaac. Thus she did not meet his bride, Rebecca, the daughter of her brother, Laban. Imagine that Sarah was still living when Rebecca became Isaac's bride. What would she have said to Rebecca? What stories would she have told? What kind of advice would she have given? Would they have gotten along well? Which of Rebecca's sons, Jacob or Esau, would have been Sarah's favorite grandchild?

↯ 8 ↯

Jacob's Blessing

Unlike the other patriarchs, little is known of the life of Isaac after the *Akedah,* the binding of Isaac, except for his marriage to Rebecca and the birth of their twin sons, Esau and Jacob. An intense rivalry developed between these brothers, as it had between Cain and Abel and between Isaac and his stepbrother Ishmael. It is clear from the biblical narrative that, while Jacob was the favorite of Rebecca, his mother, Esau was the favorite of his father. For this reason, and because Esau had been the firstborn, he was to receive his father's blessing, which was regarded as having great importance. Neither Rebecca nor Jacob, however, wanted this to happen.

The two sons of Isaac and Rebecca were twins. They were not identical twins but completely different from one another in both appearance and character. Esau, who was slightly older, had a hairy skin; Jacob's was smooth. Esau was quick-tempered and mean; Jacob was kind, generous, and lovable.

Jacob spent his time studying and learning to be a responsible and religious person. He learned to get the most happiness out of life by treating people fairly and helping to make the world a good place to live in for others as well as for himself.

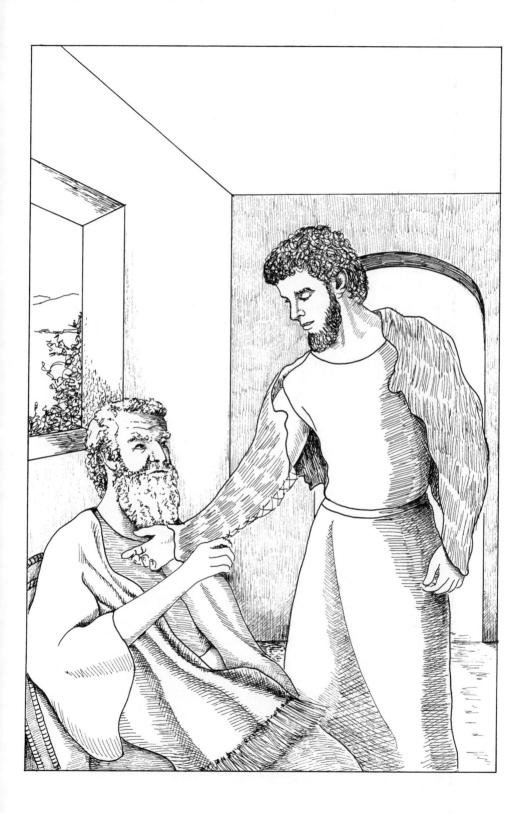

But Esau scorned anything that was good. He considered good people foolish and kindness silly. His only desire was to enjoy himself in any way he could, even if that meant hurting other people. He cared only about getting what he wanted. He could lie, steal, and even murder because he did not respect people or God.

So the two brothers had nothing in common. Esau spent all his time hunting, and Jacob studying. Most of the time the two boys went their own ways, not interfering with each other. Even their dislike for one another did not amount to much until the day their father, Isaac, explained to them the law of the "Right of the Firstborn Son."

"My sons," Isaac said to them, "there is something I must tell you. In every family the father has one certain gift to give away, and it must always be given to his firstborn son."

"Good! I am the firstborn son," said Esau, smiling.

"What is that gift, Father?" asked Jacob, trying to hide his disappointment at being the secondborn.

"The gift is called the birthright."

"What is this birthright?" asked Esau.

"It is the right of inheritance," said Isaac. "If there is property to be inherited, the older son gets it."

"Does the second son get nothing?" asked Jacob.

"Oh, yes, of course," Isaac said. "When the birthright passes to the older son, he then takes care of the younger."

"Don't worry, Jacob," Esau laughed. "I'll take care of you."

Jacob did not like that because Esau's laugh seemed to say, "Just wait, I'll be the master, and you'll be my slave."

"It means," said Isaac, explaining further, "that the older son gets the first and the best of everything."

"Well, I like that, of course," Esau said. "That'll be fine for me. I'll have a lot of fun."

"Wait, Esau," Isaac said. "It isn't only fun. Having the birthright carries with it certain serious responsibilities."

"Responsibilities?" Esau questioned. "I don't like that. What sort of responsibilities?"

"The owner of the birthright must always worship God; he must be an honorable man; he must work hard and take good care of the family."

"Huh." Esau stamped his foot. "That's not a gift. It seems more like a nuisance to me."

"It doesn't to me," said Jacob sadly. "I wish I had the birthright."

"Well, you haven't," said Esau. "Though I don't think much of it, it still belongs to me."

After this conversation, in spite of his disappointment at being the secondborn son, Jacob continued to work and study hard, and he loved his father and mother as much as ever. His mother, Rebecca, however, was unhappy because the birthright belonged to Esau, the older twin. She knew that Esau was selfish and Jacob was kind and that it was Jacob who deserved to have it. But there was nothing to be done about it. Esau was the firstborn, and the birthright belonged to him.

One day Esau was out hunting in the forest. He had already killed a bear, a deer, and two partridges. Suddenly he saw another hunter coming. It was the famous royal hunter Nimrod. Nimrod and Esau were bitter rivals in field and forest, each trying to prove that his skill was greater.

While Esau saw Nimrod, Nimrod did not see him. This gave Esau his chance for revenge on his hated rival. Hiding in some thick bushes when Nimrod and his two lieutenants passed, Esau, without warning, sprang out and, with three stabs of his spear, killed Nimrod and the two lieutenants. When he saw the three men lying dead on the ground, fearing that Nimrod's followers would find and kill him for having murdered their king, Esau ran away as fast as he could.

Finally he reached home, tired from running, dusty from hunting, and very hungry. Upon entering, Esau found Jacob in the kitchen, cooking a pot of red lentils.

"Why do you stand here and cook?" Esau asked angrily. "Why don't you let one of the servants cook for you?"

"Because I like to cook," Jacob said.

"Well then, give me some of those lentils," Esau said gruffly. "I'm hungry."

"No, I can't. These are for father."

"Why don't you cook him some tasty fish or meat? Why should you cook these cheap lentils?"

"Don't you know that lentils are a sign of mourning?" Jacob asked.

"Mourning? For whom are you mourning?"

"Our grandfather Abraham. While you were in the forest hunting, he died. I mourn for him because I loved him. He was a good and a just man."

"Oh, you're such a fool," Esau mocked, "to believe in goodness and justice."

"Then why should you want your birthright?" asked Jacob. "To keep it, you have to be a religious person. You have to believe in goodness and justice. Why don't you sell it to me?"

"I despise my birthright," Esau shouted. "It isn't worth anything! It isn't worth as much as a dish of those lentils! Will you give me a dish of those lentils for it?"

"Yes," said Jacob. "I'll give you these lentils, and, for this dish of lentils, I'll buy your birthright."

"All right," Esau said, his mouth watering. He could hardly wait. "Give me the lentils."

"Not so fast," Jacob smiled. "I know you, my brother. I want more than just your word for it. After you eat my lentils, you'll pretend you were only joking. Oh, no, brother Esau, I want some proof from you that you're really selling the birthright to me."

"All right," Esau said gruffly, angry that Jacob didn't trust him and annoyed, too, that Jacob knew him so well. "All right, then, call in two servants as witnesses. I'll write out a paper stating that I am selling you this worthless birthright."

While Jacob went for the two servants to act as witnesses, Esau sat down at the table and on a piece of parchment wrote that he was selling his birthright to his brother Jacob on that day. As he finished writing, Jacob came back with the two servants. They watched Esau sign the statement. He poured some sand on the writing so that the ink would dry quickly. Then he said to the servants, "You two sign your names here."

First one servant signed his name, then the other. Esau poured more sand on the wet ink. When the ink was dry, he rolled up the parchment and handed it to Jacob, saying, "Take it. I sell you my birthright. Now give me the lentils. I am so hungry I feel as though I were starving."

Jacob took the parchment from Esau and gave him the dish of lentils.

Esau was very careful to keep this whole matter a secret from his father so Isaac should not know that Esau had sold his birthright for a mere mouthful of food.

Now Isaac was a very old man. Having reached the age of one hundred and twenty-three years, he knew that the time for him to die was coming close. Before that time came, however, he wanted to give his blessing to his firstborn son, Esau.

Had he known that Esau had sold the birthright, Isaac would not of course, have given Esau the blessing. But, since he did not know, he called Esau to him and said, "My son, tonight is a holiday. Bring me food to eat. Prepare good food for the holiday, and I will bless you before I die. Yes, I will bless the one who is worthy of being blessed."

The only person to whom Esau showed any kindness was his father, so he said, "Very well, Father. I'll get some good food for you to eat." Then he left his father's room and went out to the forest to kill some animals.

When God heard Isaac say that he would bless "the one who is worthy of being blessed," God determined that it would not be the wicked Esau who would bring his father the food and receive the blessing.

God then called to Satan and said, "Isaac does not know that his son Esau is evil. Isaac is blind and cannot witness Esau's wickedness. Now he wants to bless Esau, but that he must not do. Esau is now going into the forest to hunt for food. You are to hinder him in every way possible. See that he finds no animals to kill. Go now, hurry."

"I'll hinder him, all right," Satan thought. "This is the sort of task I enjoy." Satan flew down to the forest where Esau was striding among the trees.

Now Esau did not care how he got the food for his father. He would just as soon steal it as not. But he did not see any animals already shot by other hunters. So he said to himself, "I guess I'll have to do my own hunting."

Very soon he trapped a deer. He tied it up and left it on the ground while he went hunting for more. Meanwhile Satan untied the deer. Off it went, leaping away to safety.

Soon, Esau trapped another deer, bound it up, threw it over his broad shoulders, and carried it to the spot where he had left the first deer. But, to his surprise, there was no deer lying there, only the rope with which the deer had been tied! He was puzzled, but he left the second deer lying on the ground, tied up with rope, and went off again to trap another.

And, again, the minute Esau's back was turned, Satan untied the deer, and it bounded away. This went on, Esau's trapping and binding the deer, and Satan's untying and freeing it, for four long, tiresome hours.

Meanwhile, at home, Rebecca said to her son Jacob, "Jacob, my son, go and prepare good food for your father. Then he will know that *you* are the worthy one, and he will bless you before he dies."

"I would rather not do that," Jacob said. "I do not want to deceive my father. He is blind and will not know that it is I, Jacob. I am sure he will have a blessing for me, too, even after he blesses Esau. Besides, if I trick him into giving me Esau's blessing, he will curse me when he discovers the trick. I do not want my father's curse!"

"If he discovers your trick," Rebecca said, "I shall take the blame for you. I will tell him that Esau is wicked and does not deserve his blessing and that you are the one worthy of being blessed. I heard the words he used. He said that he will bless the one who is *worthy* of being blessed, and that is you."

"Still, I am afraid. It will be impossible to deceive him even for a moment. You know how smooth my skin is and how hairy Esau's is. If my father touches my arm, he will know at once that I am not Esau."

"Don't let that trouble you," Rebecca said. "Look what I shall do." She took the skin of two young goats and sewed them together and made a garment to cover Jacob's smooth skin.

"There," she said. "Put on this garment of goat skins. Now if your father touches you, he will feel the hair, and he will think you are Esau."

"But it is wrong for me to do this," Jacob protested. "How can I deceive my father?"

"In this case it is not wrong. It is you who deserve the blessing. Your father does not know how wicked Esau is. It will be a sin for your father to give his blessing to someone so evil. I must prevent your father from committing this error which he would surely commit because he is old and blind. That's why I urge you to go now, get the food cooked well, take it to your father, and receive his blessing."

"But why don't we just tell my father," Jacob asked, "that Esau does not deserve his blessing? Then he will offer it to me."

"Oh, no, my son," Rebecca said. "Isaac would not believe us. When Esau is with him, he always pretends to be good. Now there is no time to convince him that Esau is unworthy. Don't be afraid. Trust me. I know that we are doing the right thing."

So Jacob agreed to his mother's plan. He prepared some good food, put on the garment made of goat skins, and went to his father's room. He knocked on the door, entered the room, and said, "Father."

"Enter," said Isaac. "Who are you?"

"It is I," Jacob said. "I have come with the food for the blessing."

Isaac thought it was Esau, and he said, "You've come in a great hurry to receive your blessing."

Jacob said nervously, "God sent me with great speed."

When Isaac heard the name of God, he suspected that something was wrong because Esau would never have mentioned God's name. He thought to himself, "I had better make sure this is Esau." Aloud he said, "Come close to me, my son, so that I can feel you."

When Jacob heard these words, he was petrified with fear. He was sure that Isaac would discover the trick. His feet turned to stone, and he could not move them. Not one inch could he move. He pulled and pulled at his feet. He strained and strained at his muscles. For the moment he was turned to stone.

And God, seeing that Jacob could not move, said, "Michael, Gabriel. Go down to Jacob and help him."

The angels flew so fast that they descended from heaven into Isaac's room in a second. Michael took hold of Jacob's left hand. Gabriel took hold of his right hand. Pushing and pulling, and pulling and pushing, they moved him forward to Isaac's chair. Then they flew back to heaven.

Isaac reached out and took hold of Jacob's hand. When Isaac felt the hairy goat skin, he said, "The voice is the voice of Jacob, yet the hands are the hands of Esau."

"Come, my father," Jacob said. "Here is some good food I have prepared. Come, eat this food." He placed the dish in front of his father.

Isaac tasted the first piece and found that it was delicious. There was, in fact, something remarkable about it. If he wanted the piece of meat to taste like pheasant, it tasted like pheasant. If he wanted it to taste like chicken, it tasted like chicken. It tasted like anything he wanted.

Isaac knew then that God had specially blessed this food. Therefore the person who brought him this food was worthy of being blessed. So he felt certain that the son standing before him was the one to whom the birthright properly belonged.

He blessed Jacob by saying, "May God give you of the dew of heaven and of the fertile places. God will give you wisdom to study the Torah. You shall love and worship God, and everyone who blesses you will be blessed himself."

Jacob thanked Isaac. He wanted to shout and sing for joy, but he controlled himself and quietly left his father's room. He hurried to Rebecca and told her about the blessing his father had given him.

Meanwhile, after four long and weary hours, Esau returned in a very bad temper because Satan had prevented him from getting any deer. His clothes were dusty from the forest and torn by bramble bushes. His hands were dirty from tying up the deer that had always escaped. His face was streaked with sand and mud. He was tired and hungry and angry.

On the way home he found a dog, killed it, cooked it, and brought it to his father. He was still so angry that when he spoke his voice was harsh and rough. He said, "Let my father arise and eat my food."

At the sound of this harsh voice, Isaac realized that this son was really Esau and that he had indeed given his blessing to Jacob. He said to Esau, "This food you give me smells bad. It smells like the flesh of a dog. The food that Jacob gave me was wonderful."

Esau's face flushed with anger, and he shouted at his father. "What did you give Jacob in return for that wonderful meal? He gave me only a dish of lentils, and for that I sold him my birthright!"

"You foolish, wicked son," cried Isaac. "Have you really sold your birthright for a mess of lentils, you evil one?"

"Yes, I did," Esau said crossly. "I was hungry."

"Hungry, you stupid one!" cried Isaac. "For hunger you sold your birthright! You despised the most precious gift you could ever own, and you sold it cheaply for a little bit of food. I was beginning to grieve that I had given your blessing to your brother Jacob, and not to you. But now I see that I gave it to the right son. He really saved me from committing a sin when he took away your blessing."

"He bought my birthright, and I kept silent," Esau said angrily. He was so excited, he shouted. "Now that he has stolen my blessing, shall I be silent now, too? Take that blessing back from him, and give it to me!"

"No, Jacob shall keep it," said Isaac. "He has proved himself to be the worthy son."

"Oh, he is not so noble," Esau sneered. "Didn't he deceive you? He tricked you into giving it to him."

"No, my son," said Isaac calmly. "The fault was not Jacob's. The fault was yours. If you had believed in God, you would not have sold your birthright. God saw that you were wicked and helped your brother Jacob get the blessing. If you had not been sinful, it would have been you who had received it."

Esau realized that he could not coax his father into taking the blessing away from Jacob. So he pretended to be sorry, and he said, "Oh, my father, take pity on me. Did you really have only one blessing? Can't you bless me, too? Can't you give me even a little one?"

These words made Isaac feel sorry for Esau. After all, he was his son, even if wicked. But, because he felt that Esau did not really deserve a blessing, he kept silent.

Then Esau began to weep. He shed three tears, one from his left eye, one from his right eye, and one remained hanging on his left eyelash. God saw Esau weeping and called to Isaac, "Isaac! Isaac! The wicked one weeps for his very life. Give him a small blessing."

So Isaac gave Esau a small blessing.

Commentary

The voice is the voice of Jacob, yet the hands are the hands of Esau.
Genesis 27:22

*   *   *

In the Bible Jacob and Esau are not judged in terms of good and bad. Jacob is described as his mother's favorite and Esau as his father's favorite. Esau is presented as a man of action and Jacob as a man of contemplation. By buying his brother's birthright and later tricking his father into believing that he is Esau to obtain the blessing of the firstborn, Jacob appears to be treading on unethical ground. In the Midrash, however, the rabbis portray Jacob as a man of purity and moral perfection, and Esau is presented as the incarnation of evil. Thus, Jewish descent is traced from the line of Jacob. Black and white portrayals such as these are characteristic of the Midrash in cases of paired characters. Such is the case also with Ishmael. In the Torah Ishmael does not attempt to harm Isaac and suffers when he is cast out into the wilderness with his mother, Hagar. In the Midrash, however, Ishmael attempts to murder Isaac by shooting arrows at him. Later Ishmael hopes that Abraham will complete the sacrifice of Isaac at Mount Moriah so that he can inherit Isaac's portion.

*   *   *

In the Midrash every detail of the biblical narrative is important. The Bible recounts that Jacob bought Esau's birthright with a bowl of red lentil soup, a soup traditionally cooked during a time of mourning. Observing this, the rabbis concluded that the house of Isaac was in mourning over the death of Abraham and that Esau had gone hunting rather than remaining at home, suggesting that he was concerned more with his hunger than with his father's grief.

*   *   *

The rabbis also seek to justify the sale of the birthright to Jacob by demonstrating the evil nature of Esau, who murders Nimrod. In the Midrash Esau openly disdains the birthright and, in the presence of two witnesses, signs a legal pledge to forfeit it. This is intended to create the impression that the sale of the birthright was valid and binding, justifying Jacob's actions. In fact, even God participates in the conspiracy to obtain the blessing for Jacob, commanding Satan to delay Esau's return from the hunt until the blessing had been given to Jacob. The rabbis viewed this affair as predestined, freeing Jacob of any guilt. Even Isaac ultimately takes Jacob's side in this version of the tale, recognizing the hand of God in the events and Esau's lack of faith.

* * *

In later Jewish texts known as Kabbalah, which interpret the Torah in a mystical way, Esau, like Cain, became identified with pure evil. In more recent times, however, certain hasidic rabbis (e.g., Nachman of Bratslav) suggested that the tale of Jacob and Esau can be seen as a parable of the struggle between people and their own souls. In such an inner struggle, Jacob represents the *yetzer tov,* the good impulse, while Esau represents the *yetzer hara,* the evil impulse.

* * *

Ironically, although the Jews belonged to a culture that honored the birthright of the firstborn, the younger sons—Isaac, Jacob, and Joseph—become the true bearers of the tradition. This indicates that, although Jews observed their laws and rituals with great care and devotion, they departed from the letter of the Law when they felt there was a compelling need to do so.

Write Your Own Midrash

When Jacob, disguised as Esau, stood before his father for his brother's blessing, Isaac was suspicious. We know this because he says, *"The voice is the voice of Jacob, yet the hands are the hands of Esau."* What would have happened had Isaac discovered that it was indeed Jacob and not Esau? How would the story have changed? How would this have changed Jewish history? Imagine the story of Jacob if this event or others were changed. What if Laban had allowed Jacob to marry Rachel without tricking him so that Jacob would have had only two sons instead of twelve. Would it mean that, instead of twelve, there would have been only two Jewish tribes? Consider the consequences if only one event in Jewish history had turned out differently.

❧ 9 ❧

Jacob and the Angel

Jacob's life involved a great many struggles. From the first he had to struggle with his brother Esau. After he tricked his father, Isaac, into giving him the blessing that had been intended for Esau, Jacob had to run away to avoid his brother's wrath. He went to live with his uncle, Laban, whom he served as a shepherd. Jacob came to love Laban's younger daughter, Rachel, and worked seven years for the right to marry her. But Laban tricked him into marrying his older daughter, Leah. So Jacob worked another seven years for Rachel. By then Jacob, who had spent fourteen years working for Laban, feared that Laban would not let him leave with his family and flocks. So Jacob and his family departed at night without telling Laban. After following and confronting Jacob, Laban finally let him go. Jacob returned home, only to find his brother Esau coming to confront him with an army. It was at this tense moment in his life that Jacob remained alone with his flocks on one side of the river Jabbok, where he was to have yet another great struggle.

Jacob lived in Haran for twenty years. During that time he had married and had many children. He had worked hard for his father-in-law, Laban. But now he was eager to return home. He was homesick for the sight of his

mother and father and for the fields and rivers and trees of Canaan.

He knew that his father Isaac, who was very old, might not live much longer. The land of his birth beckoned to him, and he felt that the time had come when he must leave Haran.

On the day he decided to return to Canaan, he told his wives, Leah and Rachel, to pack all their clothes and jewels and other possessions.

"Tomorrow," he said to them, "we shall start on a journey to Canaan."

Then he went to his father-in-law, Laban, who was also his uncle, and said, "I am going back to Canaan with my wives and with my children. For twenty years I worked for you without any wages. Now you must pay me something. I want some sheep and some goats."

"No!" shouted Laban. "You will not get anything. You don't deserve it. You came here with empty hands, and with empty hands you shall return!"

"It's true I came here with empty hands," said Jacob, "but not with idle hands." He held them out, work-scarred and rough, to Laban. "With these hands I worked very hard for you for twenty years. Never once did I ask you for wages. Even now I'm not asking for much. All I ask is that you give me the sick goats and the black sheep from your herds."

"Oh, very well," grumbled Laban. "If that's all you want. But be sure you take only the goats that are sick and the sheep that are black."

Jacob went out to the pasture and chose the sick goats and the black sheep. He had fifty goats and fifty sheep. "That makes only one hundred," he said to himself, "but I am satisfied."

Then suddenly, in the winking of an eye, other sick goats joined them, and they began to grow in number until there were three hundred thousand. So, too, the fifty black sheep mysteriously increased until they also numbered three hundred thousand. Now Jacob had a huge herd of six hundred thousand animals!

When Laban and his sons saw how magically Jacob's herds had increased from a mere one hundred to six hundred thousand, they began to plot to steal the animals from him.

However, God warned Jacob, "Jacob! Jacob! Your father-in-law plans to cheat you. Hurry, leave Haran. Return at once to your own country where you will be safe. Once you are there I will send My *Shechinah,* My Holy Presence, to shield you. Go therefore quickly to Canaan, for My *Shechinah* will not rest upon you outside the Holy Land. So hurry, Jacob, hurry."

Jacob needed no more urging, and he set out immediately—he and his two wives, Leah and Rachel; and their two maid servants, Bilhah and Zilpah; and his children, Reuben, Simeon, Levi, Judah, Dan, Naphtali, Gad, Asher, Issachar, Zebulun, and Joseph; and their herds of six hundred thousand goats and sheep. After they left Haran, they crossed the Euphrates River. They reached Gilead, and from Gilead they traveled until they came to the ford of the river Jabbok.

There Jacob sent on ahead his two wives, together with the two handmaidens, his eleven sons, and all their possessions, except for the herds of goats and flocks of sheep, which he himself planned to take across the river.

He was alone with his herds and his flocks when all at once he saw coming towards him a shepherd who had herds of sheep and camels as large as his. They too must have numbered at least six hundred thousand.

"Greetings to you," said the shepherd.

"Greetings to you," responded Jacob.

"We each have many herds to get across the Jabbok," said the stranger. "Let's work together. If we help each other, it will go faster."

"Very well," said Jacob. "But let's get my herds over first because my family is already waiting on the other side."

"Agreed," said the shepherd, and with his little finger he raised all of Jacob's six hundred thousand sheep and goats and sailed them over across the Jabbok before Jacob could even blink his eyes.

"Oh!" cried Jacob. "What magic is this?"

"It is no magic." The shepherd smiled. "Come, now you must take my herds across."

"Why don't you lift them over with your little finger as you did mine?" asked Jacob.

"No. We agreed to help each other. I helped you in my way with yours, now you help me in your way with mine."

"Very well," said Jacob. "An agreement is an agreement."

After the way his herds moved across in one instant, Jacob really expected that the herds of the stranger would be moved over magically, too. But no. Because the stranger took five sheep and five camels and led them through the ford, Jacob had to do the same. He took five sheep and five camels over across the river. Then they came back, and the shepherd took ten sheep and ten camels across the river, and Jacob took ten sheep and ten camels. Then they came back, and the shepherd took fifteen sheep and fifteen camels across the river, and Jacob took fifteen sheep and fifteen camels. At this rate, Jacob thought to himself, "Since we take five more each time, the job should not take too long."

At the end of two hours they were each taking one hundred sheep and one hundred camels across at one time. But, when Jacob looked back at the herds on the opposite shore, they did not seem any smaller than they had been at the beginning.

On and on they continued, now two hundred sheep and two hundred camels, now three hundred sheep and three hundred camels, and at the end of four hours they were taking six hundred sheep and six hundred camels across at one time. *Still* the stranger's herds seemed no smaller than before.

They took eight hundred sheep and eight hundred camels,

nine hundred sheep and nine hundred camels, one thousand sheep and one thousand camels, and six weary hours later they were taking two thousand sheep and two thousand camels over at one time. And *still* the herds seemed no smaller!

Jacob was exhausted by now, but he could not stop to rest because the shepherd kept right on taking more sheep and more camels across. They worked seven hours and eight and nine and ten, and Jacob was ready to collapse. And, when he looked at the herds still to be taken over, they seemed every bit as large as at the very beginning.

After they had worked almost the whole night long, for as many as fifteen hours, Jacob was completely worn out, and he lost his temper. He shouted at the stranger, "You wizard, you cunning wizard! What evil magic are you working?" And then he threw himself at the shepherd and started to wrestle with him.

"Ah," cried the shepherd, wrestling with Jacob. "So you want to fight me, do you? Well, I'll show you what I can do."

He touched the earth with his little finger, and fire sprang out of the ground.

"Do you think you can frighten me?" cried Jacob, wrestling all the harder.

"Now, I'm really going to hurt you," warned the shepherd, intending to wound Jacob gravely.

But, at that moment, God called, "No! No!"

And the stranger pulled back his hand before wounding Jacob.

"Who are you?" Jacob asked. "Tell me who you are."

"Never mind who I am." The stranger did not want to tell him that he was really the angel Michael. "Let's get on with our fight."

So they kept on wrestling. They pushed each other and pulled each other's arms. They jabbed each other's shoulders and bent each other's backs. But the angel Michael, thinking that God would keep him from winning this fight, touched his little finger to Jacob's thigh and injured him.

The injury hurt Jacob, and he cried out in pain, almost losing his hold on Michael.

Immediately God rebuked the angel. "Michael, Michael, have you done right in hurting My priest Jacob?"

"Your priest Jacob!" Michael exclaimed. "Is it not I who am Your priest, O God?"

"You *are* My priest in heaven, and he is My priest on earth. Michael, how dare you hurt My servant?"

"Oh, I acted in haste," Michael cried. Then he called, "Raphael, Raphael, come down and bring your healing."

In an instant Raphael flew down to earth, down to where Michael and Jacob were wrestling.

"Whom shall I heal, Michael?" Raphael asked.

"Heal this wound I made on Jacob."

"Quickly shall I heal him," Raphael said, touching his little finger to the wound on Jacob's leg. "There, I shall hold my finger on the sore for five seconds, and it will be entirely healed. Now count with me."

So Jacob and Michael and Raphael all counted together, "One, two, three, four, five."

"Oh, that feels better already," Jacob said.

"There," said Raphael. "It's all healed. Now I'll leave you." And with a mighty sweep of his powerful wings he rushed into the sky.

But neither Jacob nor the angel Michael watched him go because they started wrestling again.

And once again God called down, "You have not told Me why you have hurt Jacob, My firstborn son."

"I thought you would be ashamed of me, O God," answered Michael, "if I lost this struggle with an earthly creature. I did it only for the glory of the heavenly hosts."

"Very well, then, Michael," said God. "But you must make up for the harm that you did. From now on, you who lead the hosts of heaven must become the special guardian angel to

Jacob. Whenever he or his children cry for help, you will bring their prayers to Me."

Michael heard and knew of course that he would obey, but for the present he kept on wrestling. All over the ground they rolled, the mortal and the angel.

After three more hours of this struggle, Michael said, "I see now that you have become stronger than I. In saying that I was your guardian angel, God took away some of my strength and added it to yours. I give up this struggle. I admit you have won. So let me go, Jacob."

But Jacob held on tightly to Michael's arm. "No!"

So they continued to wrestle. Time passed. Then the night was over. The dawn came, and the day was about to begin. Then Michael said, "Now, do let me go, Jacob. It's daytime. Let me go."

"Oho," Jacob laughed, holding him more tightly. "Why are you afraid of the daylight? Only thieves or gamblers are afraid of the light because they have no place to hide. Are you one of them?"

"Of course not. I do not fear the light," Michael said. "But I must get back to heaven. It is time for all the angels to sing our morning song of praise, and it is my duty to lead the heavenly choir."

At that moment, a company of angels swooped down from the sky and stood poised at the right side of the wrestling pair; another company flew down and took positions to the left. Together, in one voice, the angels called out, "Come, Michael, come. Ascend to heaven. The time of song has approached. Come, lead our choir, or no one will sing. Come, Michael, come."

"You see," Michael said to Jacob. "The angels call me. I must go."

"I will let you go," said Jacob, "if you tell me some of the deep secrets of the world."

"Oh, no! There were angels once who betrayed the deep secrets of the world, and they were banished from heaven for one hundred and thirty-eight years. Do you want that to happen to me? Please let me go."

"If you won't tell me secrets," said Jacob, "then bless me."

"Bless you? Why should you want my blessing?"

"Because the angels once blessed my grandfather Abraham after they had visited him."

"But they were sent to Abraham for just that purpose, to bless him. I wasn't sent to bless you. Let me go, I say."

"No. You must bless me," Jacob insisted.

The band of angels, grouped around them, called again, "Michael, Michael, come up to heaven. The time of song is at hand. Without you our voices will not blend in harmony. Come, Michael, come."

"I must first bless Jacob," Michael said. "Then I shall ascend." Then to Jacob he said, "May it be the will of God that all your descendants, your children and their children's children, may be brave and generous like you. And Israel will be your name. That is my blessing."

"Why this new name?" asked Jacob.

"The name Israel means 'he who conquered the angel.' You have conquered me. Your twelve sons will be known as the twelve tribes of Israel. Now, let me go."

"Your blessing is for my children. That is good. I hope it will come true," Jacob said. "But have you no blessing for me?"

"Yes. A great honor will be yours. In time to come, your name will be joined with that of God. In all the prayers of Israel, people will say, 'The God of Abraham, Isaac, and Jacob.' That is an exceptional blessing, a wonderful blessing. Now, let me go."

Then Jacob let go of Michael, and Michael and the host of angels vanished up into the sky. Jacob was left alone. He looked closely at the river and the river bank as if to fix the scene in his mind forever.

Commentary

Jacob was left alone. And a man wrestled with him until the break of dawn. Genesis 32:25

* * *

The struggle of Jacob with the "angel" is one of the most fascinating and mysterious episodes in Jewish literature. In the text Jacob wrestles with an *ish,* a man. But this figure has been traditionally identified as an angel—either Michael or the guardian angel of Esau—or as an evil being, even Satan himself. It has even been suggested that Jacob was wrestling with himself, with his own guilt over his treatment of Esau, who was waiting for Jacob with his army on the other side of the river Jabbok. All of these interpretations make sense, for the image of the struggle lends itself to so many meanings.

* * *

The miraculous increase of Jacob's flock from one hundred to six hundred thousand was no doubt intended to represent the growth of the people Israel from a small tribe to the six hundred thousand who were said to have been present at the giving of the Torah on Mount Sinai. In the Midrash, as recounted in this tale, a magician meets Jacob at the river Jabbok and persuades him to cooperate in taking each other's flocks across the river. The magician gets Jacob's flocks across with the wave of his finger, but, for Jacob, the task of transporting the magician's large flock becomes an exhausting ordeal. Samael, the Evil One, knew that Jacob was destined to wrestle with the angel that night and weakened Jacob before the confrontation. This midrash echoes another in which Jacob wrestles with Samael himself. According to mystical tradition, Jacob wrestled with God, an interpretation indicated by the meaning of Israel, Jacob's new name: *"For you have striven with beings divine and human, and have prevailed."* (Gen. 32:29)

* * *

The use of illusion by Satan, disguised here as the magician, was, from the rabbinic view, his greatest power. Often Satan would create the illusion of wealth or of some other desirable quality to lure his victim. In one midrashic account of the binding of Isaac, Satan appears to Abraham first as an old man who tries to dissuade him from following God's command, then as a young man who tries to warn Isaac, and finally as a river that blocks their way. Abraham sees through this illusion, causing it to vanish.

* * *

In the medieval period, this theme of illusion was central to the mystical literature of the Kabbalah, as well as the central theme of many folktales. King Solomon figures prominently in some of these tales; rabbi-sorcerers, such as Rabbi Adam and Rabbi Judah Loew, are also popular figures. These rabbis use the same powers of illusion to convince evil kings to change their attitude toward the Jews or to protect Jews in danger. In one such tale a king who has threatened the Jews wakes up at the bottom of a pit, is arrested, and ordered to perform impossible tasks. He is saved through the intervention of Rabbi Adam. When the illusion ends and the king returns to his throne, he reverses the evil decree he had passed against the Jews. This legend is found in the first book of tales about Rabbi Isaac Luria, known as the Ari, who lived in sixteenth-century Safed. This book, *Shivhei Ha'ari, In Praise of the Ari,* served as the model for many hasidic collections about *rebbes,* starting with the founder of Hasidism, the Baal Shem Tov.

* * *

Jacob wrenches a blessing from the angel, echoing Jacob's earlier deception whereby he received the blessing of the first-born. In both cases Jacob manages to obtain a blessing that was not intended for him—yet, one could say that he was destined to receive these blessings all along.

Write Your Own Midrash

With whom do you think Jacob wrestled? Was it a man, an *ish,* as the text says? Do you think it was an angel or an evil being like Satan or Samael? If it was an angel, do you think it was the guardian angel of Esau? Perhaps it was Esau himself, who saw Jacob alone by the shore of the river and decided to take his revenge. The unclear text makes it an ideal subject for a midrash. Decide with whom you think Jacob was wrestling. Then write a midrash describing the encounter.

❧ 10 ❧

The Stones That Bowed Down

After all his struggles, Jacob was finally able to return to the land of his ancestors, where he raised his twelve sons and one daughter. Of all his children, he most loved Joseph and Benjamin—the two sons he had with his favorite wife, Rachel. He spoiled Joseph, giving him a splendid coat that made his brothers envious. Joseph made matters worse by telling his brothers of dreams in which they all bowed down to him. Finally the brothers sold him into slavery, telling their father that he had been killed by a wild animal, bringing back Joseph's bloodied coat as proof. In the Torah, many years passed before a distraught Jacob learned that Joseph was alive. But, in the Midrash, Jacob did not have to wait as long.

On a cool windy day, near the city of Dothan, ten men sat around a campfire. Their flocks and herds grazed nearby. The fire crackled merrily. A strong breeze stirred the sands. The men were silent. More than silent, they were ashamed. They could not look at one another. They sat staring at the fire, without saying a word.

These men were Jacob's ten sons: Reuben, Simeon, Levi, Judah, Issachar, Zebulun, Dan, Naphtali, Gad, and Asher. There were two more sons, Benjamin, the youngest who was at home,

and Joseph. It was because of Joseph that these ten brothers sat in silent shame staring at the fire.

They had just sold Joseph as a slave!

For hours now they had sat around the campfire, telling each other why they had been right in doing so cruel a thing. They reminded each other that Joseph was vain, that he was their father's favorite, and that he boasted of dreams in which he saw himself as king and his brothers as his slaves. Their jealousy of him had finally become so unbearable that today, when he followed them to the good grazing lands of Dothan where they had brought their father's flocks, they sold him to a wandering caravan of Midianites.

The Midianites had carried Joseph off towards Egypt.

Now the brothers were worried. What could they possibly say to their father to explain Joseph's absence? Then, after long hours of arguing, they had fallen silent.

Issachar finally broke the quiet. "It isn't as if we hadn't tried to get him back. Didn't Dan and Asher and Zebulun and Simeon ride after the caravan to buy Joseph back from the Midianites?"

"It wasn't our fault," Zebulun said, "that we couldn't find them."

"Those are weak excuses," said Reuben. He had been in the mountains looking for some stray lambs and so had no part in the selling of Joseph. But he was the most worried because he was the eldest son, and his father would hold him responsible. "What will we tell our father?"

"I know one thing we should not tell him," Dan said. "We must never tell our father that we sold Joseph as a slave. Let us swear to that."

"Yes," agreed Asher. "We must all swear an oath of secrecy."

"Here," said Zebulun. "Let's take Joseph's coat of many colors. Each one of us must take hold of it and swear never to tell our father."

So each one took hold of Joseph's coat, and all together they said, "We promise never to tell our father Jacob that we, his sons, sold Joseph as a slave!"

They let go of the coat, all except Reuben. He held it in his hand and said, "But, my brothers, what *will* we tell our father?"

"I have an idea!" cried Issachar. "Let us kill a goat, tear this coat, and dip it in the goat's blood. Then we'll tell our father that Joseph was killed by a wild beast—by a lion or a wolf."

"Yes, yes, let's do that," they all agreed.

They quickly gathered all their belongings—their tents and their sleeping blankets, their cooking utensils and their food. All of it they packed on the camels. Then they rounded up the sheep and the goats from the pastures. They chose a very small goat and killed it, tore the coat of many colors into shreds, and dipped it in the goat's blood.

After that was done, they began the long journey home. They traveled for one and a half days. Finally, after covering many miles, they reached the tents of Jacob.

They dismounted from their camels, and slowly all of them walked to their father's tent. Naphtali held behind his back Joseph's blood-stained coat.

Jacob stood in the door of his tent, with his little son Benjamin next to him.

"Greetings, Father," called the ten older sons.

"Greetings, my sons," said Jacob. "You were gone so long I worried about you."

"To find good grazing fields," said Simeon, "we had to go as far as Dothan this time, Father."

Jacob looked from one son to another, glad to see each one. He looked from Reuben to Simeon, from Levi to Judah, from Issachar to Zebulun, from Dan to Naphtali, from Gad to Asher.

Then he exclaimed, "But Joseph! Where is Joseph?"

"Joseph?" asked Asher. "Isn't he at home, Father?"

"No! I sent him to find you. Didn't Joseph come to you?"

Reuben stepped forward. "No, Father. We have not seen Joseph, and we too have been worried about him because of something we found. As we passed the road near Shechem, we found this."

He motioned to Naphtali, who came forward with the blood-stained coat. "We found this garment covered with blood and dust."

"That is Joseph's coat!" cried Jacob. "Covered with dust and blood! Oh, he has been killed by wild beasts! My poor son Joseph!"

The brothers hung their heads in shame. And Jacob began to weep. Little Benjamin began to cry because he was frightened. Then all the brothers began to weep because they were deceiving their father so cruelly.

Nobody could comfort Jacob. "Oh, my son Joseph," he cried. "I did love you dearly. Oh, my son, gladly would I have died for you!"

His grief was sad to see. He wept as though his heart would break. For seven days he mourned for Joseph. Then, on the eighth day, he stopped weeping and called his sons together.

"My sons, take your bows and arrows. Go out to the fields and the forests. Look for the body of Joseph. Bring me the first wild beast you find. Do not slay it. Just bring the beast to me. I will take vengeance for my son's death."

Without a word, the sons took their bows and arrows. Five went out into the fields and five into the forests. But of course they did not look for the body of Joseph. They knew he was not dead. Instead, they searched for a wild beast. The first one they saw was a wolf. They captured it and brought it to their father.

"We could not find Joseph's body, Father," said Zebulun. "But here is a wolf we trapped. It was the first wild beast we saw."

Jacob cried to the wolf, "Why did you devour my son? He did you no harm. Yet you have harmed him!"

The wolf opened its mouth and said, "I swear by the God who created me that I did not devour your son Joseph."

"What! You can speak!" Jacob exclaimed.

"Yes," said the wolf. "God has given me speech to answer you so that you may do no wrong. If you slay me, it will be unjust."

"Speak on!" Jacob cried. "Speak on!"

"I come from a country that is far away," said the wolf. "I am searching for my own little son who has disappeared. Today, when I was looking for him, your sons captured me. Now I am in your hands, Jacob. You can do with me as you like. But I swear to you that I have never seen nor harmed your son Joseph."

"The wolf speaks the truth," Jacob said. "He is innocent. Release him. Let the wolf go free."

Zebulun released the wolf, and it ran away to search for its own lost son.

Then Jacob said, "Seek no more among the wild animals. Leave me alone with my grief."

So, for many weeks and many months, the older sons left their father to find his comfort in prayer.

One day, after a whole year had gone by, Jacob said to himself, "Now I am no longer sure that my son Joseph is dead. I have mourned for him for twelve long months. Now that the year has passed, I should begin to accept the loss of my beloved son. But, even after a year, my heart is not comforted. Therefore I am beginning to believe that Joseph must be alive. I shall go into the mountains. There I may find an answer to the question in my heart: Does Joseph live?"

All this he said to himself and told no one of his plans. He put on his long, black cloak, took a chisel and a pickax, and by himself went away to the mountains. He climbed the first hill. It was small and did not take long. The next mountain was a little higher and a little steeper, and he climbed it more slowly. At the top he stopped for a few moments to catch his breath because the next mountain was still higher and still steeper. When he had rested, he slowly climbed the third mountain. Reaching its top, he rested again. Then he said, "This is the place."

He took off his long, black cloak, folded it up, and hung it carefully on the bough of a tree. Then he selected a large, smooth rock and with his ax and chisel carved out twelve stones.

On the first stone he inscribed the name of his oldest son,

Reuben. Beneath the name, he carved the sign of the first constellation in the sky called Ram, and then the name of the corresponding month, Nisan, according to the Hebrew calendar. When completed, the writing on the first stone read: Reuben, Ram, Nisan.

On each of the eleven remaining stones he wrote the name of one of each of his eleven remaining sons, the sign of the constellations in the heavens, and the names of the Hebrew months. So the twelve stones read:

> Reuben, Ram, Nisan
> Simeon, Bull, Iyar
> Levi, Twins, Sivan
> Judah, Crab, Tamuz
> Issachar, Lion, Av
> Zebulun, Virgin, Elul
> Dan, Balance, Tishri
> Naphtali, Scorpion, Cheshvan
> Gad, Archer, Kislev
> Asher, Goat, Tevet
> Joseph, Water-Carrier, Shevat
> Benjamin, Fishes, Adar

Then Jacob took eleven of the stones and stood them up in a row. The one that read Reuben, Ram, Nisan, he stood up facing the others. Then he said, "Stones, bow down before my son Reuben."

But no stone moved. They all remained upright and solid.

Jacob took the stone marked Reuben, Ram, Nisan and put it with the others. He took the one that read Simeon, Bull, Iyar and stood it in front of the others. Then he said, "Stones, bow down before my son Simeon."

But no stone moved.

Then Jacob put Simeon's stone back with the others and took the stone marked Levi, Twins, Sivan. He set that stone up before the eleven other stones and said, "Stones, bow down before my son Levi."

Once again the stones remained standing, without moving. One by one, then, Jacob took each stone named for each of his sons, stood it alone in front of the others, and asked the others to bow down before it. No matter to which stone he asked the others to bow down, the stones remained firm and did not budge.

Jacob then took the stone marked Joseph, Water-Carrier, Shevat. This stone he set in front of the others. In a loud, commanding voice, Jacob said, "Stones, if my son Joseph lives, bow down before his stone!"

As he finished saying the words, all the other eleven stones moved. Slowly they bowed down before the stone marked Joseph.

Jacob smiled for the first time in a year. He now believed that Joseph was alive, but still he wanted to be sure.

On these mountains there were cedar trees, olive trees, and palm trees.

Jacob took the stone marked Joseph and set it before the cedar trees, and he said, "Cedar Trees, bow down before my son Joseph."

The wind whistled in the trees as the branches moved. One by one the cedar trees bowed. Then they straightened up again.

Jacob then carried the stone marked Joseph to the olive trees. He placed it before them and said, "Olive Trees, bow down before my son Joseph."

As the trees began to bend their branches, the olives on their delicate stems trembled but did not fall. The olive trees slowly bowed. Then gently they straightened up, and the olives stopped quivering.

Finally, Jacob took the stone and placed it before the stately palm trees.

"Palm Trees, bow down to my son Joseph."

With great dignity the palm trees bowed down. Then they straightened up and stood erect.

"Oh, now I know that my son Joseph lives," cried Jacob. "The stones of my other eleven sons, the cedar trees, the olive trees and the palm trees have all bowed down to Joseph's stone. I know he is alive!"

Then Jacob took his pickax and chisel, put on his long, black cloak, and went down the mountains towards his home. Although he was lonesome for Joseph, he was consoled by the knowledge that somewhere in the world Joseph was still alive.

Commentary

They sold Joseph for twenty pieces of silver to the Ishmaelites, who brought Joseph to Egypt.   Genesis 37:28

*   *   *

Jacob suffered greatly upon learning that his favorite son, Joseph, had been devoured by a wild beast. The rabbis always identified with the patriarchs as father-figures, making Jacob's pain especially great. In the Torah many years passed before Jacob learned that Joseph had survived. In this midrash, however, the rabbis imagined a way for Jacob to find out after only one year. Jacob challenged first the twelve stones and then an equal number of trees (cedar, olive, and palm) to reveal whether or not Joseph was alive. In each case the stones and trees bowed down to the stone bearing Joseph's name. This legend parallels a famous story in the Talmud about Rabbi Eliezer, who had a dispute with the other rabbis about a point of the Law. He said, "If what I say is right, let this carob tree prove it," and the carob tree moved on its own. But the rabbis were not convinced. So Rabbi Eliezer asked the waters of the stream to run backward if he were right, and they did. Still, the rabbis were unmoved. So he asked the walls of the House of Study to collapse if he were correct. They started to collapse, only to be stopped by another rabbi. None of these signs made the rabbis change their minds. Instead, they insisted that the matter be decided democratically because "the Law is not in heaven," meaning that, once the

Torah was given to the Jewish people, it was for the Jewish people to interpret. In a related legend, a rabbi met Elijah and asked him how God had responded to the rabbis' refusal to acknowledge the miracles. According to Elijah, the Holy One smiled and replied, "My children have overruled Me, My children have overruled Me." (*Bava Metzia* 59b) (For a parallel story of a collapsing roof, see the commentary on "From Slave to Prince.") In this legend and in the midrash about Jacob, nature is called upon to serve as a kind of oracle. In both cases there are four tests, supporting the view that these are parallel midrashim.

✳   ✳   ✳

The tale of the speaking wolf is a vivid story with a strong moral. By being able to talk to the wolf, Jacob learns that the animal, too, has lost his son, for whom he was searching when the brothers captured him. Just as the story of the binding of Isaac announces to the world the end of human sacrifices, so this legend announces that animals, like human beings, are capable of suffering. Since Jacob had twelve sons (who fathered the twelve tribes) and there are twelve signs of the Zodiac, the legend of the stones told in this story also supplies the origin of the signs of the Zodiac, where each sign is identified with one of the twelve sons.

Write Your Own Midrash

After Joseph's brothers sold him into slavery, they had to live with a terrible secret and a lie—the secret that Joseph was alive and the lie that he was dead. Ten of the brothers knew this secret; the youngest, Benjamin, did not. Did the brothers ever reveal this secret to Benjamin? If so, did he keep the secret or let his grieving father know that Joseph was still alive? Imagine that this secret is somehow told. Describe who tells it and what happens when Jacob finds out about the terrible deception of his sons.

♦ 11 ♦

From Slave to Prince

Just as his father Jacob had faced many struggles in his life before establishing himself as the patriarchal father of the twelve tribes of Israel, so too did Joseph rise to the position of viceroy of Egypt after great hardship. Joseph's protected childhood came to an abrupt end when his brothers cast him into a pit and then sold him into slavery. Slaves in those ancient times had no rights; their lives were in the hands of their owners. As a slave in the home of Potiphar, the high priest of the Egyptian god On, Joseph distinguished himself with wisdom and honesty. However, he was cast into prison for refusing the advances of Potiphar's wife. But, even in prison, Joseph distinguished himself through his ability to interpret dreams. It was this skill that eventually brought him to Pharaoh's attention for Pharaoh was in need of someone to interpret his dreams.

Somewhere in the world Joseph was alive. That somewhere was Egypt, where he had been brought after a long journey through the desert. On the way the Midianites had sold him to a wandering caravan of Ishmaelites. And it was the Ishmaelites who brought Joseph to Egypt.

They planned to leave immediately on another journey. Since they did not want to take Joseph with them, they left him in the care of a shopkeeper.

"Take care of our slave," they said. "Don't be easy with him. Make him work hard. We will sell him when we return."

This shopkeeper was poor. His business was small and brought in only a little money. He soon learned to like Joseph and sympathized with the boy. He knew that to be a slave was hard and sad. So the work that he gave him to do was not too difficult. And Joseph performed his duties well.

Because this shopkeeper was kind to Joseph, God blessed him. Before the man even knew what was happening, his business increased as if by magic. Soon his safe was filled with gold and silver. Then the drawers in his desk were choked with money. Then the shelves became piled high with gold, and the counters were covered with silver. Very soon the shop became a treasury of precious metals.

The town people began to talk about this miracle. The tale was told from one person to another of the shopkeeper who had become rich since he had taken charge of the young slave from the land of Canaan.

The story spread far and wide, into every hamlet and city of Egypt, until finally it reached the great city of Memphis. In Memphis there lived a man named Potiphar, an officer of Pharaoh, the king. Potiphar was the third most important man in all of Egypt.

His wife's name was Zuleika. She too had heard the tale of the slave named Joseph who had brought vast wealth to the little shopkeeper. Potiphar was wealthy, but Zuleika was greedy, always wanting more gold and more treasures. She wanted this "good-luck" slave to be added to her household and to work these wonders for her.

So she said to Potiphar, "Buy me this slave Joseph."

"We have enough slaves," answered Potiphar.

"But this one will bring us good fortune."

Because Potiphar never liked to argue with his wife, to end the discussion, he sent one of his servants to buy Joseph. Now Joseph belonged to the Ishmaelites and not to the shopkeeper. He really did not have the right to sell Joseph. But the shopkeeper did not dare refuse to obey the servant of the great and powerful Potiphar. So Joseph was sold and brought to Potiphar's palace in the great city of Memphis.

When Joseph was brought to the throne room, Potiphar said, "You look strong and healthy. Your whole appearance and manner please me. Were you born a slave?"

"No, Your Highness."

"How were you made a slave?"

"They bought me in the land of Canaan. I am a Hebrew."

"I like you," said Potiphar. "You shall be my personal servant."

In the days that followed, Potiphar liked Joseph more and more. He saw that Joseph kept himself clean and neat and did his work well. But he noticed, too, that Joseph was always talking to himself.

"What are you always mumbling?" he asked him one day. "Are you trying to bewitch me?"

"Oh, no," answered Joseph. "I am praying to God to make me a good servant so that I may do my work faithfully and well."

"You Hebrews are always praying to your mysterious God whom no one can see," Potiphar said. "Why don't you pray to the gods of Egypt as I do?"

"They're not the true gods," answered Joseph. "The God I worship created the earth and everything in it and everybody on it."

"Your God cannot be as powerful as you say," Potiphar said. "But I am willing to test your God. Hand me a cup of spiced wine." When Joseph had given it to him, he said, "If your God is so faithful to you, then let this spiced wine turn into a bitter wine."

And, as he was speaking, the spiced wine became bitter to his lips!

"I shall make another test," said Potiphar. "See this yellow lily. I wish it to change into a scarlet rose."

And, as he was speaking, the color of the flower turned from yellow to red, and the lily changed to a rose!

"Good," said Potiphar. "I see that your God does have power. Can you win your God's protection for me and my household?"

"I will pray for God's blessing upon you and yours," Joseph said, "just as I did for the shopkeeper who first sheltered me."

"Good!" Potiphar exclaimed. "Then I know I shall be blessed. Now, Joseph, I will make you my chief servant. Here are all the keys of my palace." He handed Joseph a bunch of keys. "This key is for the wine cellar, this one for the flour, this for the sugar, that for the spices."

One by one, Potiphar explained to Joseph what each key was for. He was now in complete charge of Potiphar's palace. His master also gave him better food than the other servants ate, and he even arranged to have Joseph study music and painting, languages and poetry. Potiphar treated Joseph like a son instead of a servant. Joseph was so grateful that he thanked God for turning his master's heart to kindness.

But alas! The day came when false charges were made against Joseph by the evil Zuleika, who sought revenge when Joseph refused to embrace her. Thus Joseph was cast into a dungeon. There, in that dark cell, he was neglected and forgotten for a long time.

Meanwhile, Pharaoh, the king of Egypt, was troubled with disturbing dreams. For two years his sleep had been broken by nightmares. What worried him most was that in the morning he could not remember a single dream!

One night Pharaoh dreamed as usual. The next morning, when he awoke, he cried out, "This time I remember my dream! I remember it clearly! But, I do not understand it!"

He issued a proclamation commanding all the princes, the wise men, and the wizards to appear at the palace on the next morning at the tenth hour. Pharaoh had had a strange dream, the proclamation said, and whoever could interpret the dream would be crowned a prince of Egypt.

The news was spread all over the land, to the farthest corner and to the most distant city.

Long before the hour of ten on the following morning, the princes and the wise men and the wizards began streaming into the palace from near and far. They came from Goshen, Raamses, and Zoan. By the dozens they came, the rich and poor, the humble and great. By the appointed time, more than one thousand had poured into the throne room of the palace.

Pharaoh was seated on the royal throne which was set very high at the top of seventy stairs. If a prince or an ambassador came to have an audience with the king, he was permitted to mount up to the thirty-first step, and Pharaoh came down thirty-six steps. But, if an ordinary person came to see the king, that person mounted only three steps and the king came down only four steps and spoke from that distance.

If one knew seventy languages, then one could walk up every one of the seventy steps, right to the very throne. And in Egypt one could not become a full prince without learning the seventy languages of the world.

When Pharaoh saw all the princes and the wise men and the wizards from all over Egypt gathered before him, he raised his hand for silence.

"My people, I have had a strange dream. I shall tell it to you, and you will interpret it for me. The one who explains it correctly will be made a prince, and, if he is already a prince, I will add greatly to his honors."

The thousand people in the room all began to murmur at once, each looking jealously at the people standing near him, each hoping the others would fail.

"This was my dream," said the king.

"I dreamed that I saw seven fat, healthy cows come out of the river Nile and begin to graze on the river banks. Then out of the river came seven skinny, sickly cows, and these skinny cows ate up all the seven fat, healthy cows. Then I dreamed that I saw seven big, good ears of corn and seven thin ears of corn, and the seven thin ears swallowed up the seven big ears.

"Who among you can interpret this dream of mine?"

A wise man from Goshen spoke up. He walked up five stairs because he knew five languages: Egyptian, Greek, Arabic, Ethiopian, and Syrian.

"The seven fat cows, O Pharaoh," he said, "mean that you will have seven daughters, and the seven lean cows mean that your seven daughters will die."

"No," said Pharaoh. "I do not believe that this is the correct explanation."

Then a wizard from Raamses spoke up. He mounted seven steps and said, "Pharaoh, the seven fat cows are the seven kings that will rule over Egypt, and the seven lean cows are the seven princes who will revolt and conquer the seven kings."

"No," said Pharaoh. "I do not believe that explanation."

Then spoke a prince from Zoan. He mounted thirty-one steps, and Pharaoh descended thirty-six.

"Pharaoh," said the prince of Zoan. "The seven good ears of corn mean that you will conquer seven countries, and the seven lean ears mean that those seven countries will rebel against you."

"No," said Pharaoh. "That cannot be the true meaning."

One by one, the princes and the wise men and the wizards tried to explain the king's dream. And, one by one, they failed. Seven hours passed, and fifty people had spoken.

Pharaoh then said sternly, "I command that all who have spoken falsely shall be killed by the spear!"

The fifty people grew faint with terror, and all the rest murmured in fear.

Then the king spoke again. "Can it be that there is no one in my kingdom with enough wisdom to interpret my dream?"

Then Potiphar spoke up. "Pharaoh, I have a slave, by name Joseph. He is a Hebrew and worships a mysterious God. This Joseph is very wise about dreams. I believe he could interpret the dream of Pharaoh. At present he is in the dungeon."

"Bring this Joseph here!" commanded Pharaoh. "The wise men who spoke will be spared if this Joseph succeeds. Of course, the fifty doomed people prayed that Joseph would interpret the dream correctly.

When Joseph was brought into the throne room, he mounted the first three steps.

Pharaoh said, "Slave, tell me truly what my dream means. Even if it is something sad, speak without fear. Say nothing merely to please me. Speak only the truth."

"Pharaoh," said Joseph, "I really cannot interpret dreams. These things are in the hand of God. Only if it is God's wish, will I be able to explain your dream to you."

"Then listen to my dream," said Pharaoh, and he told his dream to Joseph. When he finished, he said, "Now I hope your God will help you explain it to me."

"Pharaoh," said Joseph. "Your dream begins happily but must end sadly. For seven years Egypt will be rich and prosperous and have plenty of all foods to eat. But, after those seven years of plenty, there will come seven years of misery and poverty, starvation and famine."

"Famine! Horrible!" murmured one wizard.

"Starvation! Awful!" whispered a prince.

All the princes and the wise men and the wizards murmured against Joseph.

"Quiet!" ordered Pharaoh. And everyone fell silent. "Now Joseph, how can you prove that your interpretation is right? What sign can you give me?"

"Let this be a sign that my words are true," said Joseph. "Your wife, the queen, will have a baby in two hours, a little boy. While you are rejoicing over the news of his birth, you will be told that your other son, now two years old, has died."

"We shall see," Pharaoh said. "But meanwhile you will wait in the dungeon of the palace."

Joseph was taken from the throne room to the dungeon.

Two hours later the queen had a little baby boy, and the whole court celebrated the happy event. While everyone was dancing and drinking and rejoicing, a nursemaid brought Pharaoh the sad news that his two-year-old son had just died.

Pharaoh began to weep for his little son. Then, after a while, he dried his tears and called all the princes and the wise men together. He said to those assembled before him, "You heard Joseph's interpretation of my dream. Now I believe it to be true for the sign he gave me unfortunately came to pass, and my little son has died. But I must put aside my own grief. Now we must find a way to save our country from starvation after the seven years of plenty have passed. To do this we must find someone wise to be our prince. He must protect us from famine. Do you all agree?"

"Yes," said one wizard. "We must save Egypt from starvation."

"Yes, yes," said a wise man. "We must choose a very wise prince."

"Very well," said Pharaoh. "I know just the man. Joseph! Indeed, if we searched from one end of Egypt to the other, we would not find anyone as wise as Joseph, who interpreted my dream when all of you had failed. The spirit of his God is in him, and his heart is filled with wisdom. If you all agree, I will make Joseph our prince."

"Oh, no," murmured one counselor. "You cannot take a slave from the dungeon and make him our master!"

"Oh, no," said another. "Surely, Your Majesty, you remember our Egyptian law: No man may be our prince unless he speaks all seventy languages."

"How many languages does Joseph know?" asked still another counselor. "Only his own, I wager, and Egyptian."

"Send for him," suggested one of the princes, "and see if he knows any languages besides his own and Egyptian."

"Very well," said Pharaoh. He turned to a guard and said, "Bring Joseph to me tomorrow at the tenth hour. Then we shall examine him and see how many languages he knows."

Down in the dreary dungeon, Joseph was preparing for sleep. The rough plank on which he was to sleep was hard and uninviting. Still, it had been an exciting day, and he was tired.

Suddenly, to his amazement, an angel appeared.

"I am the angel Gabriel. I have come to teach you the seventy languages of the world so that tomorrow morning, when you appear before Pharaoh, he will appoint you viceroy, the highest prince in Egypt."

"Viceroy! Seventy languages!" cried Joseph. "I would like to be viceroy, but how can I learn seventy languages in one night? It's absolutely impossible!"

"You have deserved the special blessing of God," Gabriel said. "Since you must learn all seventy languages to be viceroy, you will be given the power this very night to learn any language in an instant."

"In an instant!" exclaimed Joseph. "What a miracle!"

"Come, there is no time to waste. We have seventy languages to learn. First we will study Ethiopian."

"Ethiopian," said Joseph. As he said the word—he knew the whole language in one instant! "Go on," he cried. "I now know the Ethiopian language."

"Syrian is next," said Gabriel.

"Syrian!" said Joseph, and—in the next instant he knew Syrian! "Go on," he cried. "This is marvelous. I know the Syrian language!"

"Babylonian," said Gabriel.

"Babylonian!" said Joseph. And—in that second he learned the language! "Go on, go on, I now know Babylonian," he cried in excitement.

So it was with Aramaic, Greek, Hindi, Arabic, Persian, and all the other languages of the world. The moment Joseph spoke the name, he knew the language! So, in seventy minutes he learned seventy languages—something no one has ever done before or since.

"Now my task is done," said Gabriel. "Now go to sleep and dream in all the languages. Farewell." He flew out the window.

The next morning when Joseph was brought into the throne room by the guard, he boldly mounted all the seventy steps since now he knew the seventy languages of the world. Right up to the royal throne he climbed.

"He knows seventy languages!" cried one prince.

"Then he is wise enough to rule over us," said a wizard.

Pharaoh raised his hand for silence, and said, "Joseph, you know the seventy languages of the world. Your God has given you the wisdom to rule over Egypt. There is no one here as wise as you. You will be second in command over the whole land. I am first; you are second. Whatever you say, the people will do. You will be their ruler. You are my prince."

On Joseph's head, Pharaoh placed a golden crown, and Joseph, the slave, was crowned viceroy of Egypt.

Commentary

And Joseph said to Pharaoh, "Pharaoh's dreams are one and the same: God has told Pharaoh what He is about to do."

Genesis 41:25

* * *

Jacob is often described as clever. His son Joseph also demonstrates some of this natural intelligence, first as a slave with the shopkeeper, then with Potiphar, and later with Pharaoh. Another Jewish legend tells how King Solomon, who was forced to become a wandering beggar, likewise succeeds in every undertaking. In this way the rabbis link Joseph and Solomon for they have much in common: Both were blessed with unusual wisdom and served as great rulers—Joseph as viceroy of Egypt, Solomon as king of Israel. Other key figures are also linked—Abraham and Moses, among the patriarchs, and Sarah and Rebecca among the matriarchs. (See the commentary on "The Sheltering Cloud.")

* * *

The miracles of the spiced wine that turns bitter and the yellow lily that becomes a scarlet rose are tests to prove the existence of God. These resemble the miracles that occur to Jacob in "The

Stones That Bowed Down" (see the commentary on that story). A similar test is described in a tale concerning the Emperor Rudolf II and Rabbi Judah Loew of Prague. The emperor insists on having the patriarchs and their offspring recalled from the other world so that he could see what they look like. The emperor threatens to punish the Jews if Rabbi Loew refuses his request. With no other choice, Rabbi Loew invokes a vision of the patriarchs, who appear to be of immense size. When the emperor sees one of Jacob's sons leap over the tall corn, he laughs, and the vision ends. At that moment the corner of the roof above the emperor begins to collapse, and only Rabbi Loew's intervention keeps it from crushing the emperor. (*Sippurim* I)

* * *

The incorrect interpretations of Pharaoh's dream by his soothsayers are actually additional ways in which, according to the rabbis, Pharaoh's dream could be read. The multiple explanations are like the midrashic legends themselves, which interpret the text of the Torah in numerous ways.

Write Your Own Midrash

Joseph was a great interpreter of dreams. The Midrash contains a great many dreams. While attributed to the patriarchs and sages, they were probably the dreams of the rabbis. Try to remember a dream that you had; write a midrash in which you imagine how Joseph might interpret your dream. You may find by doing this that you learn something new about the meaning of your own dream because the method used by Joseph is similar to modern dream interpretation.

✣ 12 ✣

Brothers Again

Out of jealousy Joseph's brothers sought to destroy his life, selling him into slavery. But, by a strange twist of fate, Joseph became, instead, the second most powerful man in Egypt. His brothers found themselves bowing before him, just as his childhood dreams had prophesied. Of course, at first Joseph's brothers did not know that the powerful viceroy they stood before was their brother, and Joseph was in no hurry to reveal his identity. Although he longed to be reunited with his family, Joseph also intended to settle a score with his brothers. While his vengeance was mild compared to theirs, he gave them good cause to worry before he unveiled the truth.

Joseph was only seventeen when his brothers had sold him as a slave. For many years he had worked hard for his master, Potiphar. Then, after eighteen years of slavery, he became a prince of Egypt.

He lived in a huge palace. He wore costly garments. He ate the rich foods that princes eat. Everyone in Egypt, except the king, bowed down to him. Whatever he commanded the people to do, they did. They gave him all the homage anyone could have.

During the famine about which Joseph had warned Pharaoh,

it was Joseph who saved Egypt. Throughout the seven years of plenty, when the earth produced more food than the people could possibly eat, Joseph taught them how to store the grain in the huge storage places he had built. When the seven lean years came, the Egyptians, because of Joseph's planning and saving, did not starve. So the king heaped more and more honors upon him, as he so rightfully deserved.

But, with all his honors and happiness, Joseph never forgot his father Jacob and his brothers. He was often quite homesick for them.

One day he said to himself, "I bear my brothers no grudge. I am no longer angry with them. In fact, if they had not sold me as a slave, I would never have become a prince in Egypt. But, with all my wealth and power, I am lonely for my family. I wish I could see my brothers once more."

It was during the great famine that his opportunity to see them came. The famine had spread to other countries, too. In Phoenicia, Arabia, and Palestine no one had stored grain during the years of plenty as Egypt had because they didn't know the famine was coming. Now the people in those lands were starving. Joseph knew this.

"My family in Canaan must also be suffering from hunger," he thought. "They must be saved. They must be helped. I shall let the people of other lands know that Egypt has enough corn and wheat and grain to supply every country. Then perhaps my brothers will come here to buy corn, and I shall be able to see what kind of men they have become. If I find they have lost their spite and anger which prompted them to sell me as a slave, I will reveal myself as their brother. I will forgive them, and we will be brothers again."

Therefore he sent a proclamation to all the surrounding countries:

The proclamation of His Majesty, Pharaoh, the king of Egypt, and of his prince, the viceroy of Egypt: There is grain to be bought in Egypt. To anyone desiring to purchase grain in Egypt is this order given: No slave nor servant may he send, only his very own sons.

At each of the four gates of Egypt, Joseph stationed two guards. It was their duty to take down the name of every foreigner who came to buy corn or wheat or grain. These lists of names were to be given to Joseph every evening. In this way he would know when his brothers arrived.

A few weeks later, on examining the lists one evening, Joseph saw the names of Reuben, Simeon, and Levi on the list of the North Gate. On the list of the South Gate were written the names of Judah, Issachar, and Zebulun. On the East Gate list appeared the names of Dan and Naphtali; Gad's and Asher's names were on the list of the West Gate.

"Here at last are the names of my brothers," he said. "I wonder why they entered at separate gates. Why didn't they all come in at one gate?"

He then commanded every storage place where corn was sold to be closed, except one. Thus his brothers would have to go to that one station, and he would know when they came to purchase their supply of corn. He gave orders to his soldiers that, when the men named Reuben, Simeon, Levi, Judah, Issachar, Zebulun, Dan, Naphtali, Gad, and Asher came to buy corn, they were to be arrested and brought to him.

Joseph waited one day, and the brothers did not come. He waited two days, and still they did not come. He waited three days, and, when they had not yet come, he sent his servants to find them.

They searched every road in Goshen and every lane in Raamses, but the servants were unable to find the brothers. Then Joseph decided that they must be somewhere in the great city of Memphis. So he sent groups of sixteen soldiers in a house-to-house search for his brothers.

After hunting in almost every house in the city, finally, in a poor tumbledown inn, the soldiers found the ten brothers. They were arrested and brought before Joseph in the throne room of his palace.

Joseph knew that they would not recognize him. Eighteen years ago when they had last seen him, he had been a young boy. Now he was a grown man with a black beard.

He was seated, like a monarch, on a golden throne. He looked splendid in his velvet court robes, and the large gold crown on his head shone with the reflection of its jewels. He pretended not to understand Hebrew. Joseph spoke to them in Egyptian, with his son Manasseh as the interpreter.

Joseph opened the interview by saying, "Who are you?"

Manasseh translated the question into Hebrew. Issachar answered, "We are all sons of one man in Canaan, whose name is Jacob."

Joseph interrupted him. "Ah, you are Jacob's sons, are you? Tell me, is your father still alive, and is he well?"

The brothers looked at one another in astonishment. Why should the viceroy of Egypt ask about their father's health? Then Zebulun said, "Yes, thank you. Our father is alive and in good health."

"Why have you come here?" asked Joseph.

"To buy grain and corn," answered Reuben.

"You say you've come to buy corn," Joseph said, "but your actions are suspicious. For three days you have been here, and you have made no purchases. I believe you are spies."

Reuben answered, "We are not spies, Your Majesty. We did indeed come to Egypt to buy corn."

"Your actions were not those of honest men," said Joseph. "Three of you entered by the North Gate, three by the South, two by the West, and two by the East. Why didn't you all enter the city by one gate?"

Zebulun explained, "Our father told us not to enter the city by the same gate. Because we are all strong-looking men, he feared that, if people saw us all together, they would be jealous of our strength and harm us."

Joseph nodded. He agreed with his father because indeed his brothers were strong, tall, and handsome.

"It is important for us to buy corn, Your Highness," Judah said. "Our people are hungry. But, we have an even more important task here in Egypt."

"Our father Jacob had twelve sons," Levi said. "The youngest one, Benjamin, is at home. The other one disappeared many years ago, and we are looking for him. We believe he has been sold as a slave in Egypt, and now we are trying to find him."

"Suppose you find your brother?" asked Joseph. "Suppose he should be a slave? What if his master asks a tremendous price for him, say a thousand pieces of silver? Would you pay that much for him?"

In one voice the brothers answered, "Yes!"

"What if his master refuses to sell him?" Joseph asked.

"Then we will slay the master," said Gad, "and rescue our brother."

"Then," Joseph said, pretending to be angry, "you must truly be spies. You've just admitted to me that you've come to kill Egyptians."

"No, no," Reuben cried. "We haven't come to kill Egyptians. We just want to find our brother Joseph. We prefer to do it peacefully. We would use force only if necessary."

"Hmm." Joseph pretended to be thinking. "I don't believe this story of a lost brother. In fact, I don't believe you have an old father living. I don't believe you have a younger brother, Benjamin."

"Oh, it is all true," Reuben said.

"If it is all the truth, and you are not really spies," said Joseph, "then one of you must go home and bring your brother Benjamin here. Then I may believe the rest of your story."

But the brothers refused. It was bad enough, they said to

each other, that they had been so wicked as to sell Joseph as a slave many years ago. They were not going to endanger Benjamin.

"Will you bring your brother Benjamin here so I may see him?" Joseph asked.

"No!" the brothers all said.

Then, pretending that he was still suspicious of them, Joseph had them put into jail for three days. At the end of that time he had them brought back, and he said to them, "I will permit all of you to return home except Simeon."

"Why me?" cried Simeon. "Why keep me?"

"If I keep you here," answered Joseph, "then, in order to rescue you, your brothers will have to bring Benjamin here so I can see him."

"Very well," said Asher. "We will leave Simeon with you."

The other brothers agreed.

"You may do as you wish," Simeon said to his brothers. Then he boasted, "But I'd like to see anyone throw me into prison if I resist!"

Joseph ordered seventy of his strongest fighters to throw Simeon into jail, but, when they tried to take hold of him, he let out a loud shout like the roar of a lion. The seventy men were so frightened, they fell to the floor. Then they and the rest of Joseph's servants, terrified at Simeon's shouting, ran away.

But Joseph and his son Manasseh stood their ground. "You do not frighten us," said Joseph. "Manasseh will take care of you."

Manasseh hit Simeon on the back of the neck, put chains on him, and took him off to jail. All the brothers were amazed, Simeon was the most surprised of all. He said, "This Manasseh cannot be an Egyptian. With such strength, he seems more like one of us."

Joseph smiled to himself but said nothing.

"Come," Levi said to his brothers. "There is nothing we can

do but leave Simeon here. We will go home and bring Benjamin back with us. Then we can rescue Simeon and continue our search for Joseph."

They were then permitted to buy grain and corn, which they piled onto their camels. Then they started for home.

When they were gone, Joseph took Simeon out of prison and treated him like a guest. This surprised Simeon, but being treated like a guest was much better than being in jail, and he did not ask for explanations.

Then Joseph began to wait for his brothers to return with Benjamin. He knew that his father Jacob would refuse to let Benjamin go. He also knew exactly how much corn and grain the brothers had bought to take home. When that was used up, they would have to come back for more, or they and their people would starve. He knew that sooner or later they would have to return, and he had warned them, "Do not return to Egypt without Benjamin!"

So Joseph waited. He waited one month, two months, three months, and still the brothers did not return. The days lengthened into weeks, and the months passed. Finally, at the end of the seventh month, the brothers returned to Egypt. With them was Benjamin.

All the brothers were brought to Joseph in the throne room. Judah said, "This is our brother Benjamin. Our father has sent you a letter in which he assures you that we are not spies, that we have come only to buy corn. He begs you to send Benjamin back with us. He has already lost one son and could not bear to lose Benjamin as well."

Then each brother came forward with the gifts that Jacob had sent to Joseph. They put them at the foot of the throne. Gad brought honey as solid as stone. Reuben brought the oil of almonds. Levi presented Joseph with pistachio oil. Each brother gave Joseph something that could not be found in Egypt and was, therefore, a welcome gift.

"I thank you for these gifts," Joseph said, "Now, I want you all to dine with me." He picked up a large silver cup and looked into it as if it were magical. "Judah is king of you all," said Joseph. "Let him sit at the head of the table. Reuben is the firstborn son; the second seat is his. Levi is priest; let him take the third seat."

The brothers were astonished that he knew so much about them. But Joseph, still gazing into his cup, told each one where to sit until he came to Benjamin. Then he said, "As for Benjamin, let him sit next to me."

While they were eating, Joseph picked up the cup again and said to Benjamin, "Look into this magic cup. Tell me what you see."

Benjamin looked into the cup and whispered in excitement, "*You* are my brother Joseph!"

"Yes. I am Joseph, your brother, but do not tell the others yet. First I wish to test them to see if they are really sorry for what they did to me many years ago."

"I know they are sorry!" said Benjamin. "I can tell you that."

"Still, I wish to test them fully," Joseph said. "Listen to my plan: When they are ready to go home, I will let you go with them. Then I will command them to be arrested, and I will take you away from them. If they are willing to risk their lives for you, that will prove that they are sorry for what they did to me."

Benjamin knew that the brothers were sorry. Because he was certain they would pass the test, he agreed to the plan.

When the meal was finished, the brothers prepared to go home. While they were packing their camels with the corn, grain, and wheat they had bought, Joseph slipped a silver cup into Benjamin's sack without anyone seeing. Then he said good-bye to the eleven brothers, and they started for home.

Just as they passed through the city gates, Manasseh, Joseph's son, caught up with them.

"Halt!" he commanded.

They all stopped.

"One of you is a thief," Manasseh said. "A silver cup was stolen from my father."

"My brothers and I are not thieves," cried Gad.

"We have not stolen your silver cup," said Issachar.

"Let him search our bags," Reuben suggested. "He will not find the cup. Then he will know we are honest men."

The other brothers agreed. Manasseh, starting with Reuben's, began to search their bags. He knew the cup was in Benjamin's, but he pretended to look in all of them. When he came to Benjamin's bag, he put in his hand, pulled out the cup, and held it high for all the brothers to see.

"Oh, you thief," Asher shouted at Benjamin. "You have brought shame to us all."

"Is stealing a cup as serious a crime as selling your brother as a slave?" Benjamin asked.

The brothers bowed in embarrassment and did not answer.

"Come," Manasseh said gruffly. "Don't stand here quarreling. You must all come back to the viceroy with me."

So they turned their camels around and went back to Joseph. As they came into the throne room, they all bowed down to him. He was reminded of the dream he once had of eleven stars bowing down to his star. But, even while their backs were bent, Judah muttered to his brothers, "I am so angry, I'm going to talk right up to this Egyptian."

Judah rose and stood facing Joseph. The other brothers stood back in silence.

Joseph, pretending to be angry, started the quarrel by saying, "Why did you steal my cup? Did you know it was magical? Did you think it would help you find your brother Joseph?"

"We are not guilty of stealing," Judah said proudly. "Yet we know that we are not completely innocent. Because of the sin we once committed in selling our brother Joseph as a slave, now we have been caught together, and we must all suffer alike."

"You think then that your misfortunes are God's punishment?" asked Joseph.

"Yes."

"Then, if you are really being punished for selling Joseph, why should Benjamin suffer? He had no part in that wicked sin. I will keep Benjamin here."

"No!" cried Judah. "We promised our father not to return without Benjamin!"

"What is a promise to men like you?" Joseph said. "I have learned by magic that your lost brother, Joseph, did not steal and brought you no shame. Yet, years ago you yourselves sold him as a slave and lied to your father, saying that Joseph was devoured by a wild beast. Now you can just as easily tell your father that Benjamin is a thief. Go, tell your father that Benjamin has gone as Joseph has gone, that the rope follows after the water bucket."

"Our brother Benjamin is no thief!" cried Judah.

"Don't be angry," said Joseph. "I do not accuse all of you of theft. Only Benjamin, who stole the cup. He shall stay with me. The rest of you may return to your father in peace."

"Peace!" cried Judah. "You have destroyed the peace of our family. And I shall use force, if necessary, but I shall rescue Benjamin!"

Then Joseph, pulling Benjamin with him, ran into a room behind the throne and locked the door.

"Open up!" Judah shouted. "Open up, or I'll break down the door."

The door stayed locked, and Judah continued to shout. Then he pounded against the door with his shoulder again and again, and crash—the door splintered and flew open! Judah and his brothers stood in the doorway facing Joseph and Benjamin.

"I demand justice," Judah said, "according to the law of our own country. By our laws a thief may be sold as a slave only if he cannot make good his theft. But, if he is able to pay, he must pay double for what he has stolen. We are ready, we are willing to pay double for your silver cup. Now release Benjamin!"

"No," said Joseph. "I shall not release him."

"You are breaking a promise," Judah protested. "Didn't you order us to bring our brother Benjamin that you might see him? But it is as a slave you wish to keep him. If it's only a slave you want, take one of us. Reuben is older than Benjamin, and I am stronger. Take Reuben. Take me. But let Benjamin go."

"No."

"Then take warning, Viceroy," Judah threatened. "Take warning. Once in bygone years, two of us destroyed a whole city for the sake of our sister Dinah. What do you think I will do for Benjamin's sake? If I utter one sound, destruction will cover this land as far as its very boundaries. In this country, Pharaoh is king, and you are prince. But, in my country, my father is king, and I am prince. If you do not let Benjamin go, I'll destroy you first, then Pharaoh."

Joseph remained unalarmed. He signaled to Manasseh, who stamped his foot on the ground so hard that the whole palace shook. The brothers looked at each other in surprise.

"Only a member of our family can shake a palace with one stamp of his foot," Judah marveled. "Again this Manasseh has surprised us by his strength." Then he tried to plead again. "Your Highness, why do you treat us like this? Other people of other countries have come to Egypt to buy corn. You have not embarrassed them. Why us?"

"First you threaten, and now you plead," said Joseph. "It seems to me that you are talking too much. Reuben, Simeon, and Levi are older than you. Let's hear what they have to say. Why do you do all the talking?"

"Because I shall suffer the most if Benjamin does not return with us," answered Judah. "I promised our father Jacob that I would take the whole blame if Benjamin fails to come home."

"You didn't worry about Joseph when you did not bring

him home," said the viceroy. "Yet he had done nothing wrong. But Benjamin stole my cup. I am weary of this discussion. Go home. Tell your father that the rope follows after the water bucket, and he will understand."

"I see there is nothing you understand but violence," cried Judah. "We will destroy Egypt. Come, my brothers, let us tell this Egyptian what we can do. I will raise my voice and destroy the cities."

"I will raise my arm," said Reuben, "and crush the land."

"I will raise my hand," said Simeon, "and ruin all the palaces."

"I will raise my sword," said Levi, "and slay everybody."

"I will ruin it like the city of Sodom," said Issachar.

"I will ruin it like the city of Gomorrah," said Zebulun.

"I will make it a land of ghost cities," said Dan.

Joseph listened patiently to the threats of his brothers. Then he decided that it was his turn to show his strength. He pushed his foot against the massive marble throne; it toppled over, breaking into hundreds of little pieces.

"This man is as strong as I am," said Judah.

By that time Joseph had decided that he had sufficiently put his brothers to the test. Now he was satisfied that they were willing to risk their lives for their brother Benjamin and that they surely regretted their crime of long ago. So gently this time he said to Judah, "Who told Benjamin to steal my cup?"

But it was Benjamin who spoke, careful not to reveal that he knew that the viceroy was their brother Joseph. "No one told me to steal it. Nor did I steal it."

"Can you swear," asked Joseph, "that you did not steal the cup?"

"I make an oath upon the truth," answered Benjamin, "that, just as I had nothing to do with the selling of my brother Joseph, so is it true that I did not steal this cup."

"How can I tell that your oath is a true one?" asked Joseph.

"I named my own sons for my brother Joseph," Benjamin answered. "That should prove how much I loved him. My father has suffered enough. I beg you not to bring any more sorrow on him."

Those gentle words influenced Joseph to forgive his brothers completely. And he said, "You sold your brother, and I bought him. Now I shall call him, and you may see him." So Joseph began to call, "Joseph, son of Jacob, come here. Come, speak to your brothers!"

The ten older brothers looked at all the doors, expecting to see Joseph come through one of them. But no one came into the room. And Joseph said, "Why are you looking at the doors? Look at me. Behold! I am Joseph, your brother!"

These surprising words came as a shock. The brothers began to crowd back, away from Joseph.

"Yes, it is Joseph," cried Reuben. "He will have his revenge upon us!"

"And now he is the viceroy of Egypt," cried Asher. "He has been mocking us all this time!"

"Wait, my brothers," Joseph called to them.

"I never dreamed he was Joseph," cried Dan, trying to protect Judah.

"Don't be afraid of me," Joseph begged. "I'm not angry with you anymore. I won't hurt you. If the ten of you could not destroy me, how then can I destroy ten? I have been truly lonesome for you, my brothers, and for my father. I want to be your friend again."

Then Reuben called out to the others, "He speaks the truth. Forget your fear. He has forgiven us. Let us all be brothers again." He walked forward to Joseph, threw his arms around him, and kissed him.

When the other brothers saw that no harm came to Reuben, they knew that Joseph had indeed forgiven them. One by one they came forward and embraced him. After Reuben came Simeon, then Levi, then each brother in turn.

Tears turned into laughter, grief to joy, and for hours the twelve brothers talked together in friendship. They told Joseph everything he wanted to know about Jacob, their father. Then he had to tell them of his adventures: how the Midianites sold him to the Ishmaelites who left him with the shopkeeper, how the shopkeeper sold him to Potiphar, and how finally he had become the viceroy of Egypt.

After a while, Joseph said, "I know you must all return home now. Promise me that, with your wives and your children and our father Jacob, you will all come back to Egypt to live with me."

"Perhaps it is not safe to tell our father that Joseph is alive," said Issachar. "The shock may harm him. He thinks Joseph is dead."

Reuben answered, "I think our father has always believed that Joseph is really alive."

"But it may still be a great shock to him," said Dan, "if we just blurt out the news."

"I have an idea," said Asher. "You all know how beautifully my daughter Serah plays the harp and how she makes up her own songs. We will tell Serah to take her harp to Jacob's tent and sing these words: 'Joseph, my uncle, lives. He rules over all of Egypt. Joseph, my uncle, lives.' Perhaps our father will hear the song without listening too closely, but then gradually he will begin to realize the meaning of her words."

"A splendid plan," cried Joseph. "And now, my brothers, before you go, I have some presents for you."

To each brother Joseph gave a wonderful chariot like the one in which he rode when he was made viceroy. "In these chariots," he said, "you will bring your families back to Egypt."

He gave them a special chariot for his father. To his brothers he gave one hundred pieces of silver for each of their children and beautiful clothes for their wives, also precious jewels and perfumes. When they were ready to leave, Joseph, with Manasseh at his side, rode to the gates of Egypt with them.

At the end of three months Jacob, his sons, and their families came to Egypt, and there, with Joseph, they lived in contentment for many years.

Commentary

For though Joseph recognized his brothers, they did not recognize him.   Genesis 42:8

* * *

Since the rabbis looked upon the biblical patriarchs as forefathers, the terrible treatment of Joseph at the hands of his brothers was of great concern to them. The rabbis record in the Midrash several factors which are clearly intended to lay the groundwork for Joseph's ultimate forgiveness of his brothers. The rabbis sought to make the motives of the brothers' coming to Egypt more complex, involving not only the purchases of grain in a time of famine but the search for their lost brother Joseph. This search serves as a kind of repentance as does the harsh treatment Joseph gives his brothers before he reveals his true identity. In addition, the Midrash, as reflected in this tale, shows the brothers regretting their past and revealing their feelings of guilt. This too serves to make their repentance and Joseph's forgiveness more authentic. (*Genesis Rabbah* 91:7)

* * *

Note also that the biblical account of Joseph's treatment of Benjamin when the brothers arrive in Egypt differs considerably from that found in this midrash. In the Bible Benjamin is treated like the rest of his brothers, except that his portion is larger than theirs. (See Gen. 43:34.) In the Midrash Joseph hands Benjamin the cup, which is later hidden in Benjamin's sack. When Benjamin peers into it, he learns from its magic that the Egyptian is Joseph. He then reminds the brothers of their crime against Joseph—in which, of course, he alone had not participated. In this way Benjamin, closely identified with Joseph as the only sons of Rachel, is able to voice the accusations that Joseph, who seeks reconciliation, cannot. In fact, Benjamin speaks as the voice of the rabbis, making it clear that the act of his brothers had not been forgotten, nor fully forgiven.

* * *

There are other instances in the Midrash of the rabbis speaking through one of the characters. For example, in the Midrash about the binding of Isaac, Satan is said to appear to Abraham in the guise of a devout old man, saying to Abraham, "Have you gone crazy? Are you really going to murder your son?" So great is their horror of human sacrifice that the rabbis speak here through Satan.

Write Your Own Midrash
In the legends of the Midrash we are able to discern the voices of the rabbis in the statements of some of the characters. For example, the boy Abraham first accuses his mother of abandoning her infant before he reveals that he is her son. Imagine a situation in which someone finds out that something questionable is being planned and argues that it not be done. For example, Benjamin might be following his brothers and overhear their plan to throw Joseph into the pit and sell him into slavery. As the voice of Benjamin, what would you say to the conspiring brothers? Someone might overhear Rebecca and Jacob planning to deceive Isaac. What would they say to them about this?

Selected Bibliography

ORIGINAL SOURCES IN ENGLISH TRANSLATION

Ben-Amos, Dan, and Mintz, Jerome R., trans. and eds. *In Praise of the Baal Shem Tov (Shivhei Habesht)*. Bloomington: Indiana University Press, 1972.

Braude, William G. *The Midrash on Psalms (Midrash Tehillim)*, 2 vols. New Haven: Yale University Press, 1959.

Charles, R.H., ed. *The Apocrypha and Pseudepigrapha of the Old Testament*, 2 vols. Oxford: Clarendon Press, 1913.

Charlesworth, James H. *The Old Testament Pseudepigrapha*, 2 vols. Garden City: Doubleday, 1983 and 1985.

Danby, Herbert. *The Mishnah*. London: Oxford University Press, 1938.

Epstein, I., ed. *The Babylonian Talmud*. London: Soncino, 1939.

Freedman, H., and Simon, Maurice, eds. *Midrash Rabbah*. London: Soncino, 1939.

Friedlander, Gerald. *Pirke de-Rabbi Eliezer*. New York: Hermon Press, 1970.

Gaster, Moses. *The Chronicles of Jerahmeel* or the *Hebrew Bible Historiale (Sefer Hazichronot)*. New York: Ktav, 1971.

_____. *Maaseh Book of Jewish Tales and Legends*, 2 vols. Philadelphia: Jewish Publication Society, 1934.

Glick, S. H., trans. *En Jacob: Aggadah of the Babylonian Talmud*, 5 vols. New York: Hebrew Publishing Co., 1921.

Goldin, Judah, trans. *The Fathers According to Rabbi Nathan (Avot de-Rabbi Nathan)*. New York: Schocken, 1924.

The Holy Scriptures. Philadelphia: Jewish Publication Society, 1955.

143

Noah, Mordecai Manuel, ed. and trans. *The Book of Yashar (Sefer Hayas-har)*. New York: Hermon, 1973.

Odeberg, Hugo. *Enoch Three,* or the *Hebrew Book of Enoch*. New York: Ktav, 1970.

Sperling, Harry, and Simon, Maurice, eds. *Zohar,* 5 vols. London: Soncino, 1931–34.

The Torah: The Five Books of Moses. Philadelphia: Jewish Publication Society, 1962.

SECONDARY SOURCES

Ausubel, Nathan, ed. *A Treasury of Jewish Folklore*. New York: Crown, 1948.

Barash, Asher, ed. *A Golden Treasury of Jewish Tales*. Tel Aviv: Masada, 1965.

Bialik, Chaim Nachman. *And It Came to Pass: Legends and Stories about King David and King Solomon*. New York: Hebrew Publishing Co., 1938.

Bin Gorion, Micha Joseph, and Bin Gorion, Emanuel, eds. *Mimekor Yisrael: Classical Jewish Folktales*. 3 vols. Bloomington: Indiana University Press, 1976.

Buber, Martin. *The Tales of the Hasidim*. New York: Schocken, 1947–48.

Cohen A., *Everyman's Talmud*. New York: Schocken, 1975.

Finkelstein, Louis. *Akiba: Scholar, Saint, and Martyr*. Philadelphia: Jewish Publication Society, 1962.

Freehof, Lillian S. *The Bible Legend Book,* 3 vols. New York: Union of American Hebrew Congregations, 1948, 1952, and 1954.

Gaer, Joseph. *The Lore of the Old Testament*. Boston: Little, Brown, 1952.

Gaster, Moses. *The Exempla of the Rabbis*. New York: Ktav, 1968.

Gaster, Theodor, ed. *Myth, Legend and Custom in the Old Testament*. New York: Harper & Row, 1969.

Gersh, Harry. *The Sacred Books of the Jews*. New York: Stein and Day, 1968.

Ginzberg, Louis. *The Legends of the Jews,* 7 vols. Philadelphia: Jewish Publication Society, 1909–35.

Glenn, G. Mendel, ed. *Jewish Tales and Legends*. New York: Hebrew Publishing Co., 1938.

Goldin, Hyman E. *The Book of Legends,* 3 vols. New York: Hebrew Publishing Co., 1938.

Kasher, Menachem M. *Encyclopedia of Biblical Interpretation,* 9 vols. New York: American Biblical Encyclopedia Society, 1980.

Lauderbach, Jacob Z., trans. *Mekilta de-Rabbi Ishmael,* 3 vols. Philadelphia: Jewish Publication Society, 1935.

Nahmad, Hayim Musa, trans. *A Portion in Paradise and Other Jewish Folk Tales.* New York: Norton, 1970.

Noy, Dov. *Folktales of Israel.* Chicago: University of Chicago Press, 1969.

———. *Moroccan Jewish Folktales.* New York: Herzl, 1966.

Rappoport, A. S. *Myth and Legend of Ancient Israel,* 3 vols. London: Gresham, 1928.

———. *A Treasury of the Midrash.* New York: Ktav, 1968.

Scholem, Gershom. *Kabbalah.* Jerusalem: Keter, 1974.

———. *Major Trends in Jewish Mysticism.* New York: Schocken, 1964.

Schwartz, Howard. *Elijah's Violin & Other Jewish Fairy Tales.* New York: Harper & Row, 1983.

———. *Gates to the New City: A Treasury of Modern Jewish Tales.* New York: Avon Books, 1983.

———. *Miriam's Tambourine: Jewish Folktales from around the World.* New York: The Free Press and Seth Press, 1986.

Spiegel, Shalom. *The Last Trial.* Philadelphia: Jewish Publication Society, 1967.

Urbach, Ephraim E. *The Sages: Their Concepts and Beliefs,* 2 vols. Jerusalem: Magnus Press, 1975.

Vilnay, Zev. *Legends of Jerusalem.* Philadelphia: Jewish Publication Society, 1973.

Wiesel, Eli. *Souls on Fire: Portraits and Legends of Hasidic Masters.* New York: Random House, 1972.